"Dating was your idea."

"The wedding-date part was my idea. Melissa thinks we were dating in New York. I didn't plan to lie to anyone."

"Just mislead people then."

Elizabeth had just opened her mouth to counter—did this count as bickering? "I think," Elizabeth said, "that I have a solution. For the dishonesty."

He was all ears. Contrary to appearances, Mark hadn't wanted to lie to anyone either. Something about his dad just brought out his worst judgment.

"We have five days—well, four now, really— until the wedding. As long as we go on a few dates between now and then, we're not exactly—" she lowered her voice "—*lying.*"

Mark felt himself nodding.

"Though that does require you to—" she lowered her voice again, this time with faux gravity "—*spend time with me.*"

He felt a smile kick at the corners of his mouth. "I think I can handle that."

Could *she*?

Kate Keedwell is a debut novelist and longtime romance novel enthusiast. When she's not reading or writing, she enjoys spending time with her family, playing with her dog and visiting new places. While she's lived in Illinois, Edinburgh and New York, her home state of Massachusetts will always have her heart.

Books by Kate Keedwell

Love Inspired

A Wedding Date for Christmas

Visit the Author Profile page at LoveInspired.com.

A Wedding Date
for Christmas

Kate Keedwell

LOVE INSPIRED
INSPIRATIONAL ROMANCE

LOVE INSPIRED®

INSPIRATIONAL ROMANCE

Recycling programs for this product may not exist in your area.

ISBN-13: 978-1-335-59705-2

A Wedding Date for Christmas

Copyright © 2023 by Katherine Herron

For questions and comments about the quality of this book, please contact us at CustomerService@Harlequin.com.

Love Inspired
22 Adelaide St. West, 41st Floor
Toronto, Ontario M5H 4E3, Canada
www.LoveInspired.com

Printed in U.S.A.

Finally, brethren, whatsoever things are true, whatsoever things are honest, whatsoever things are just, whatsoever things are pure, whatsoever things are lovely, whatsoever things are of good report; if there be any virtue, and if there be any praise, think on these things.
—*Philippians* 4:8

For Suzy and David, the most inspiring couple I know. Your love, faith and encouragement mean the world to me.

Chapter One

There was nowhere like Herons Bay during the holidays. Elizabeth Brennan reminded herself of this truth as she met the familiar faces and curious glances strewn about Main Street with her cheeriest poise. *Positive thoughts. No place like home and all that.* She lifted her gaze to the colored lights twinkling along the storefronts of her hometown. And breathed. *Hello, cool New England air. Hi there, Christmas spirit.*

She could almost dismiss the questions lurking beneath her former classmates' and neighbors' warm welcome-home's. The pointed looks at her ringless left hand.

Elizabeth wished she could make a formal announcement: *No, I don't mind that my high school sweetheart is marrying my childhood best friend this weekend. It's been almost ten years, and I'm really, really fine with it.*

Only, that would reek of minding very, very much. She was happy for Andrew and Melissa. She just didn't want to be an object of pity. So, she smiled at the residents strolling through town this moonlit evening and continued on her way.

She had someone to meet, after all.

Hurrying down the sidewalk, she focused on the shop windows: the miniature candy-cane-adorned Christmas tree surrounded by boxes of chocolate at Sweet Somethings, the holiday novel display at Blue Heron Books, the poinsettia bouquets and pine wreaths at Beach Rose Blooms.

Elizabeth paused at the last storefront without meaning to. Had Andrew and Melissa ordered their floral arrangements here? What flowers had they chosen for the ceremony? Growing up, Melissa had dreamt of a hydrangea-filled wedding, but were they in season now?

Elizabeth shook herself. Not her concern—even if signs of Melissa and Andrew's upcoming nuptials seemed to burst through their hometown like fresh blooms, begging for attention.

When she finally pushed herself onward and opened the door of the local coffee shop, Coastal Café, it seemed fitting that the speakers would croon a tune about coming home for Christmas.

I'll be home for Christmas, indeed.

Toasty peppermint-scented air greeted her within. Glancing around, she tugged the sleeves of her sweater into her lavender-lotion-slick palms. A nervous tic. She released them only to find herself tucking her hair behind her chilled ears instead. *Another* nervous tic.

Stalling for time, she considered the holiday menu before ordering a mint tea from the woman working at the counter—no one she knew, thankfully, though she looked around Elizabeth's age. The conversation she was about to have would be awkward enough without anyone from her past witnessing it.

Deep breaths as she paid. One then another. And then

she pushed herself across the quiet café to a table in the back corner. A lone dark-haired man occupied it. He hadn't seen her yet. Right then, he was still paging through a creased paperback, furrowing his brow, the sleeves of his Henley pushed around his forearms. He took a sip of his coffee without glancing at his cup.

The same Mark Hayes she remembered from adolescence, focused as ever.

One more calming, centering, holiday-spice-scented inhale—*Please, Lord, guide me through this*—and then Elizabeth was brandishing her brightest smile. The theater girl smile she'd honed through twenty-some-odd years of shows and auditions. It felt a bit heavier than it had back in high school, the last time she'd spent any time with Mark.

"Mark," she said, lifting her hand in greeting. "Hi."

He stilled. Before closing his book, he folded his napkin into a makeshift bookmark to save his place. Then he looked up at her. She had forgotten how arresting his eyes were. Had she ever noticed the cool blue of them? Had he ever turned them on her long enough, truly, for her to itch under their scrutiny like this? She'd glimpsed him in church earlier, but only briefly. Only long enough to come up with this idea.

"Long time, Brennan," he said. So simply. He nodded toward the chair across from his tacit invitation.

Elizabeth had heard through the town grapevine that he'd earned a PhD in English Lit earlier this year. That tracked. She could imagine a lecture or seminar room full of students eager to impress him, to warm the frost in his gaze into admiration.

Oh, nerves were making her babble, even in her own head.

"Thanks for doing this," she said. "Can you believe

we've both lived in New York for years, and it took coming home for us to meet up?" The words burst forth like a just-shaken seltzer.

Mark tilted his head. "It's a big city."

"Oh, I mean, of course, I just—"

"And I've never been sure of the etiquette on hanging out with my cousin's ex-girlfriend. Or my ex-girlfriend's best friend, for that matter."

Elizabeth kept her smile pasted on, rather than let it slip. Even as she took a mental tally of who else occupied the café (not many people this near closing time) and who was close enough to hear (no one in the immediate vicinity). She gave silent thanks that Mark had chosen such a secluded table.

"I…" she floundered.

Luckily, the barista chose that moment to call her name.

"That's me," she said. "I'll be…"

It wasn't like her to trail off, to escape from a conversation midsentence, but Elizabeth felt herself doing exactly that. She turned away from the table and headed to the counter. She should have known that Mark wouldn't force pleasantries, that he wouldn't act like her invitation to grab coffee today was anything but bizarre.

Yes, they had spent the majority of their teenage years in the same social circle. But not as friends. Occasionally as rivals, when it came to classes and grade point averages. Mostly, however, it was Andrew and Melissa who'd linked them. Andrew Hayes—Mark's cousin and Elizabeth's boyfriend from freshman year of high school through freshman year of college. Melissa Kent—her best friend since birth and Mark's high school sweetheart.

They'd gone on double dates, attended school dances and lived in each other's orbit for years without ever choosing to. And Elizabeth was fast remembering why. Mark Hayes was cold and aloof and had never seemed to like her very much. When they hadn't been competing in class, he'd given her the politeness expected from a best friend's boyfriend—or toward a cousin's girlfriend—and nothing softer.

He didn't owe her pleasantries anymore. She wasn't anything to him now that Andrew and Melissa were getting married. Which made her reason for asking him to coffee today all the stranger.

Thanking the barista for her tea, Elizabeth inhaled its heat before returning to Mark. He hadn't picked his book back up. Instead, he was watching her as though she were a particularly convoluted thesis statement.

Before reclaiming her seat, Elizabeth silently recited one of her favorite passages from Philippians to herself, one that she often turned to when she felt this on edge. *Be careful for nothing.*

It was possible that when Paul the Apostle had written those words, he hadn't been thinking of asking your teenage rival to pose as your date to your childhood best friend's wedding to your high school sweetheart.

Taking a too-hot sip from her mug, Elizabeth turned a level gaze on Mark.

"Look," she said, "I know we've never been…close. And that you've always thought I'm a little too cheery. And annoying. Maybe more than a little. But that's beside the point."

Mark opened his mouth, but Elizabeth kept going. "I promise I have a reason for asking you to meet tonight."

Curiosity glinted in his narrowed eyes. "I assumed it had to do with the wedding."

A flush traveled across her skin, warming her neck

and cheeks. So straightforward. So to the point. Why couldn't she do that? For all her rehearsing last night, actually broaching this idea was harder than she'd anticipated. And she'd anticipated it being pretty hard.

"I'm worried the reception will be awkward," she admitted.

That, incredibly, got a half smile from him. "Elizabeth Brennan, voted Most Likely to Succeed by our senior class, awkward?"

She didn't believe in rolling her eyes—too rude—but found herself tempted now. "Oh, please, you of anyone should know I can feel plenty awkward." No one back in their high school days had ever unsettled her like he had. Had ever seemed as immune to her sunny smiles.

Elizabeth expected a flippant reply, but he turned earnest. "Never seemed it to me."

"Oh." Huh. "Thank you?" She shook her head and carried on. "I did have a—well, a thought. On how to make it less awkward."

"Not go?" Only the return of that half smile told her he was joking.

"Barring that…do you need a date?"

Mark stilled at the question—the last thing he expected her to say. He didn't remember Elizabeth as much of a class clown, but she must have developed quite the sense of humor over the years. Asking him to coffee out of the blue. Showing up rambling and uncharacteristically nervous, as though she'd arrived late to an audition. And now, asking him if he had a date to Melissa and Andrew's wedding?

Strange how life worked out sometimes. It wasn't

every day that your golden-boy cousin married your high school girlfriend.

That wasn't a kind way to think of Andrew. Mark knew that. Andrew was more than just his cousin, after all; he had also been his best friend growing up. Mark was thankful for that old friendship. Missed it. The fact remained, however, that everyone had always preferred him to Mark. Teachers. Parents—his own included. The entire town of Herons Bay. And certainly women.

Case in point: the woman casting a hopeful glance at him over her mug. To be fair, everyone in Herons Bay knew that Elizabeth Brennan had only had eyes for Andrew from the time they were all kids. Plenty of their high school class had assumed they'd get married after college.

Andrew himself used to say he would marry Elizabeth one day. No one had predicted that they would break up early in their freshman year of college, the distance too much of a strain on their relationship. Not even Mark, cynic that he was.

He examined Elizabeth more closely. Beneath the lip gloss and carefully done eye makeup, the performer's smile he recalled from the community theater productions she and Melissa had done in high school, he could see cracks. A slight waver to her smile. This week must be weighing on her, too. Who got married on Christmas Eve anyway? The holidays were stressful enough without a wedding thrown in.

Sympathy, however, didn't temper the absolute ludicrousness of what she appeared to be suggesting.

"Are you asking me out, Brennan?"

Her natural blush had long burned through whatever powder she wore on her cheeks.

"Before you say no," she started. "I've been praying a lot, and I keep coming back to this idea."

He felt his brow lift. "The idea being that God wants me to take you to this wedding?"

She ignored his snark. "I'm not asking you on a real date."

Yeah. He'd figured.

"But…" she continued, "aren't you getting weird looks, too? Like you're the sad single ex from a Hallmark movie, home from the soulless city, heartsick over Melissa and Andrew's wedding? I feel like half the town expects me to break out into a rendition of 'On My Own' any second."

Mark stared.

"Les Mis," she clarified.

"I know the song. I'm just picturing it."

Back in high school, Elizabeth had spent an annoying amount of time belting show tunes—in the car as the four of them drove to dinner dates, in Melissa's basement when the four of them had studied… Her bursting into song now didn't seem out of the question.

Another blush, as if she could read his mind. "I'm not sixteen anymore."

Neither was he. Obviously. But being home like this could sure play mind games with a person, as he'd become all too aware since moving back into his childhood bedroom a few weeks ago. Coming home for a month or two to job-hunt had been the practical choice. The financially prudent call. Once he'd graduated with his PhD, once his apartment's lease had ended, once he'd realized a full-time job in academia wasn't fast-coming, he couldn't refuse his parents' hospitality.

Didn't make it any easier to find himself back home

struggling to find employment with the PhD he'd spent the bulk of his twenties earning. Or to live under the microscope of his dad's criticism and his mom's worry again. He was proud of his accomplishments, grateful for the joy he'd found in the pages of the classics and at the front of a lecture room. The person he'd become. He just didn't know how to be that person here in Herons Bay, surrounded by his past.

"Honestly," Elizabeth said, prompting him back to the present, "a date to Melissa and Andrew's wedding wouldn't make your life any easier?"

Mark shrugged. "I try not to pay attention to town gossip." A survival tactic for those who were suddenly living with their parents in their late twenties, struggling to find a job. Not that Elizabeth Brennan would know anything about that.

She deflated. "I'm not *trying* to, I just…"

She's just not used to this town's pity, Mark thought, not unkindly. Why would she be? Everything had come easily to her growing up. The top marks he'd fought her so hard for, she'd earned between theater rehearsals and performances. No doubt adulthood had treated her just the same.

"I usually like being home," she said finally, softly. "But these last couple days have been hard."

The vulnerability softened him a bit. "And spending time with me sounded easier?"

That got a small sad smile from her. "It's better than people assuming I'm still pining after my high school boyfriend. Even my parents…"

Mark winced. Town gossip, he didn't care about. Parental expectations, though…

He shook himself.

"I'm sure there are at least seven guys from high school who would trip over themselves to take you. Why not ask one of them?"

She blinked. "That's an oddly specific number." Then she shook her head. "I guess I just thought we were in the same boat." She sighed. "My mistake."

Guilt gnawed at his gut. She'd been open with him. Honest. That didn't mean he owed her the same, though.

Elizabeth took what appeared to be the last sip of her tea and then reached into her purse. A second later, she was uncapping a pen, scribbling something on her napkin and sliding it across the table to him, her stencil-neat handwriting inked across it.

"My phone number," she said as if he might have mistaken the numbers for coordinates or code. "In case you change your mind. It was nice seeing you again, Mark."

She was gone, gliding out of the café with measured steps and perfect posture, before he could call her on the lie.

Chapter Two

Elizabeth walked home with her shoulders frozen stiff and her heart hanging heavy. She had so much to be thankful for: loving parents, good friends, an adorable dog, two roommates with a shared baking habit. Currently, the luxury of walking the few blocks home from Main Street in the dark without worrying she'd forgotten her personal alarm. Blessings large and small.

So what if Mark had turned her down? He was a grump anyway, even surlier than she remembered from school. Asking him to the wedding had been a silly idea to start with, no matter how inspired she'd felt after seeing him in church this morning.

Still, it was hard not to feel—tonight, lately, for a while now—like every time she *tried*, she failed. Just look at all the fruitless theater auditions she'd accumulated to prove it.

She thanked God for redirecting her thoughts to the festive lights and decor strung around town. Happy things. The decadent white lights at the Jacobses', the jolly inflatable Santa at the Wilsons', the elaborate nativity scene at the Gowens'… And then, of course, her family's home.

She turned at the familiar Bayside B&B sign and up her parents' long driveway. Colored lights adorned the roof and framed the doorway of the colonial-style house that her parents had converted into a bed-and-breakfast nearly a decade earlier. Right after Elizabeth had graduated from high school and moved to New York. Lit up at night like this, you couldn't miss it for a mile.

Couldn't miss the cars filling the driveway, either. The guests. Elizabeth felt her heart turning leaden again. Her childhood home was usually a retreat for her, but not with every spare room filled by a wedding guest.

Typically, her parents closed for the holidays. A small beach town on the South Coast of Massachusetts wasn't exactly a hopping December tourist destination. Summer, when guests could take advantage of the sandy beach a seashell's toss away, and autumn, when they could enjoy New England's changing leaves, brought the bulk of her parents' guests.

But Melissa and Andrew's wedding was a game changer. This year, they were booked to capacity through Christmas. Anyone with a wedding invitation but no place to stay in Herons Bay—namely, college friends of the couple—had booked one of the B&B's cozy quilted beds.

It wasn't the vacation she'd planned when she'd taken this week off from work. Still, Elizabeth was glad for the chance to help her parents—even if that meant overhearing one guest whispering to her spouse that she must be *the ex* while she'd checked them in.

Andrew's ex-girlfriend? Melissa's ex-friend? Elizabeth hadn't known which the woman had meant and had relied on years of acting classes to keep her smile steady. She longed for the anonymity of New York. No one knew or cared about her romantic past there. But Herons Bay had a long memory and little new drama to dilute hers, however many years old it might be.

Elizabeth had spent her whole life, from her first childhood theater production on, aiming for the spotlight. The stage. But not like this. She didn't know when she'd be able to unwind with the house so full—to let her mouth relax from their stage smile and her shoulders from their pin-straight posture. For sleep, she supposed, exclusively. The last thing she wanted was gossip about how she looked tired or melancholy. As Mark had reminded her, their peers had once voted her Most Likely to Succeed. Was it so bad that she wanted to live up to those expectations? To seem as happy and successful as everyone assumed she'd become?

Yes, she reminded herself. Pride was not good. Pride was a trap. One that tended to snag her.

Elizabeth straightened the slump from her shoulders as she stepped onto the porch. She opened the front door, unintentionally jostling her mom's homemade cranberry wreath. Immediately, a little ball of tricolor fur launched itself at her, twirling in circles at her feet.

"Hi, Mary Tyler Morkie," Elizabeth said, squatting to give her a dog a thorough head scratch of a hello. Mary Tyler Morkie yipped a greeting, leaning into the touch.

The tiny Maltese and Yorkshire terrier mix had been a trooper about both the train ride from New York and her relocation this week. She had immediately taken it on herself to act as the B&B's professional greeter, with all the charisma of her seventies sitcom actress namesake. Luckily, all their guests so far seemed to like dogs— or at least eight-pound hypoallergenic ones like MTM.

The house stretched out silently before them, the

guests either having retired early or gone out to dinner. No sign of her parents, which meant no evening arrivals tonight. They'd be sitting in the living room otherwise, with keys and a plate of freshly baked cookies awaiting any new guests.

Gathering her dog to her chest, Elizabeth walked through the living room and up the stairs to the wing of the house that her parents reserved for family use. She could swear that the mantle had sprouted a new nutcracker or two since she'd left for town earlier. Her parents had really decorated to the nines this year. To the nineteens, even.

She patted a knock on the door. "It's me."

Her mom stood in the threshold a moment later clad in an oversize red sweater and reindeer pajama pants. Her hair—the same honey blond as Elizabeth's—was pulled into a messy bun. Behind her, Elizabeth's dad appeared to be snoring on their bed.

"Your nose is scarlet," her mom said, concern quick to crease her brow. "Are you chilled to the bone?"

"It's not that bad out," Elizabeth lied, still tucked into her favorite pink puffer coat.

"I still don't see why you couldn't have taken the car into town." Her mom ushered her inside. "Your dad and I weren't going anywhere tonight."

"I like walking. It got me to ten thousand steps today, and I got to see all the Christmas lights up close."

"Oh, those lights. They're beautiful, aren't they? Did you pass the Kents' house? They outdid themselves this year. I wonder if they'll take wedding photos there."

Elizabeth nodded, although she hadn't seen the lights at Melissa's childhood home. Then she pointed at her dad's dozing form. "Should I go?" she whispered.

"The man can sleep through anything. He's sleeping through my show."

Her mom's favorite soap opera was paused on the television screen. Elizabeth recognized the actress's face as one she'd seen since elementary school, when she'd first started to catch glimpses of *Pine Harbor*—named for its harbor setting and perpetually pining characters. She wondered if that was the career the actress had envisioned for herself. If she'd ever done anything else. If she ever wanted to do anything else.

Had Elizabeth? She still remembered the first stage show she ever saw. Her parents had taken her to a touring production of *Cinderella*, playing at a local theater. Even then, as a little kid, she'd immediately wanted to sing and dance across a stage like that someday. As she grew older, she only fell harder into that dream. To act was to step outside your own experience, to become someone else and take the audience with you. What compared to that? If she'd ever had another dream, she'd long forgotten it.

Growing up, she'd filled her after-school-hours with the Cranberry Players, Herons Bay's community theater group. In college, she'd continued acting in as many shows as possible. Thus far, she'd devoted her adulthood to Broadway auditions. What else was there for her to do but keep trying? Keep auditioning? Otherwise, all those years of work, all the encouragement from her parents, not to mention her arts degree, would prove a waste.

She would prove a waste.

Bleak thoughts. Elizabeth turned from the television, and from her insecurity, and claimed one of the comfy hydrangea-blue armchairs that occupied the sitting room of her parents' suite. Mary Tyler Morkie nestled in happily, flopping onto her back.

"We've barely gotten to spend time together since you got home," her mom lamented, taking the adjacent chair. "The B&B is never this busy outside of July."

"It's okay," Elizabeth assured her. "I knew that things would be chaotic here with the wedding."

A Christmas Eve wedding. Was it selfish if a tiny part of Elizabeth resented Melissa and Andrew for stealing this holiday from her? For taking time she could have spent relaxing with her parents and filling it with guests' needs instead? Oh, she knew her parents appreciated the business. And she understood the reasoning, the sentimentality behind Melissa and Andrew's Christmastime wedding. They'd started officially dating near Christmas almost ten years ago now. The "Our Story" section of their wedding website had recounted the whole tale, but Elizabeth remembered it well enough on her own.

At the time, she and Andrew had only broken up a month earlier, over Thanksgiving break. Though the hurt had long scarred over, a pale ghost of past pain, she could still summon the surprise that had stabbed her when she'd realized how quickly he'd moved on. And with whom.

"I know, I know," her mom said. "It's still a shame, though. We never get this much time with you over the holidays."

"We have time now," Elizabeth countered, trying for her usual sunniness.

Guilt nibbled at her. Up until recently, she'd nannied for a pair of girls on the Upper West Side, and their parents had paid her a considerable bonus to help out over the holidays. She'd needed the money too much to take more than a day or two off for Christmas. And the Carmichaels had done so much for Elizabeth—hiring her right out of school, providing her with a room in their luxurious town house, understanding when she swapped shifts with other nannies in their circle to make time for auditions and open calls. Was it any wonder that she'd hated saying no to them?

Plus, she adored her charges, Ophelia and Juliet. Their Shakespearean names had seemed a sign from God when she'd first heard about the job—and, indeed, Mrs. Carmichael was quite the theater fan.

Elizabeth shook herself back to the present. She still babysat for the Carmichael girls from time to time. But at a certain point, she'd needed a job that offered health insurance. Hello, barista apron and latte art. She'd hoped, by now, that she might have obtained healthcare through the Actors' Equity Association. But that dream was beginning to feel loftier and loftier. Sure, there had been small successes here and there, but nothing big. Nothing steady. Nothing she could build a future on.

"We'll get to enjoy the wedding as a family, at least," her mom resolved with a light sigh. "Unless…you have a date on his way from the city?" Her smile turned brighter. "I could let a date steal you away."

Too much hope in her mom's voice. Too difficult to explain that between her auditions and shifts and babysitting gigs, she didn't have the *energy* for a relationship right now. Let alone the time. Let alone the bravery. She already risked her heart with every audition; it couldn't take any more fractures.

"I don't think Melissa would appreciate me springing a surprise guest on her five days before the wedding." Which was exactly why Mark would have made such a convenient option.

Her mom waved that off. "She's your oldest friend. She owes you a plus-one. Now, who could *I* set you up with…?"

Elizabeth leaned over to grab the remote from the coffee table. Mary Tyler Morkie opened one disapproving eye at the disruption. "Hey, let's turn your show back on."

Her mom meant well, but she didn't realize the dread that the prospect of a blind date with one of her old classmates unspooled within her. She didn't want to face any fellow alum's disappointment—maybe even satisfaction— when he realized that Elizabeth Brennan, perennial overachiever, hadn't achieved her dreams. No stage career to speak of. A job that she could do just as easily here (and more happily) at the local café. No reason for her to have ever left Herons Bay.

Mark, she could have stood. Mark had never bought into her good press. And Mark had looked so uncomfortable in church today at the congregation's curious glances. Exactly like she felt.

"Point taken," her mom said, lifting her hands in surrender. "I'll drop it. As long as you help me figure out if Priscilla here has actually returned from the dead or if this is her long-lost twin."

Giving silent thanks for the respite, Elizabeth quipped, "Or if she's a ghost."

"That's the spirit, sweetheart."

Mark's childhood bedroom felt small. Smaller, somehow, than the bedroom of his tiny Manhattan apartment. Maybe it was the twin bed from his adolescence. Or the desk on which he'd once constructed social studies dioramas and AP exam study guides. The living memory of it all.

Or, Mark suspected as he sorted idly through his teen-age bookshelf, maybe it was the booming sound of his father's voice easily audible from downstairs. He'd just begun to page through a C. S. Lewis paperback when he heard his uncle's equally boisterous voice join in. Hard to tell whether they were cheering for the Bruins or cursing the other team for scoring on them.

He'd never expected to live here again. Academia was competitive, no question there, but he'd hoped to have something lined up by the time his apartment's lease ended. Alas, his first round of applications hadn't yielded an offer. He wasn't alone in that—several of his cohorts were still searching, too, though some of them had found adjunct or temporary positions for this year.

Mark hadn't. Until recently, he'd been working at a bookstore in New York, but when his apartment's lease had ended, it hadn't made sense to re-sign. Who knew where he would wind up working? During this round of job applications, Mark had applied for any open position in any literature department, regardless of the location.

Maybe he'd return to New York. Maybe he'd get a position here in New England. Possibly, he'd move to Nebraska or New Orleans. It was up to God where he landed. He'd done all he could, polishing his teaching and research statements, submitting application after application. How else could he prove to his parents that he hadn't wasted years of effort and time?

"Mark!" his uncle called upstairs. "You up there?"

He couldn't hear his mom's voice, but he could imagine her downstairs, assuring his uncle Brad—Andrew's dad—that Mark was indeed home tonight, and, oh, weren't they excited to have him back? He could practically hear his father's noncommittal grunt of reply, too.

Mark abandoned the paperback and followed the sound of his uncle's voice. Down the garland-lined staircase. Into the living room, where his dad and uncle sat on the leather couch watching the New England Sports Network while his mom curled up in the adjacent armchair with her e-reader.

"Mark!" his uncle cheered at his arrival, as though he'd just slap-shot the Bruins' puck into the opposing team's goal. "Come join us. My house has been so busy with the wedding that I've barely gotten to see you since you moved home."

Moved home. It sounded permanent when put like that. Mark resisted the urge to correct his uncle.

"Good to see you," Mark said instead. "Big week, huh?"

His uncle shook his head. "My son. Just had to plan a Christmas Eve wedding. I tell you, Gina is out of her mind trying to keep up with all the planning. She's home right now, going over the seating chart one more time. Those cousins of hers take some careful arranging."

Mark wondered where his aunt had slotted him. At a singles table? With his parents? Andrew had graciously explained by text message, shortly after proposing last year, that he wouldn't want to put Mark in the awkward position of standing as a groomsman.

Mark's sweater felt too tight. Too hot.

"You didn't RSVP with a plus-one, did you?" Brad asked, squinting.

His dad gave a gruff laugh. "Does that dissertation of his count?"

Mark had never learned how to force a laugh, so he left his answer at a headshake. Nope.

"No girlfriend in the Big Apple?" his uncle continued. Mark prayed for the Bruins game to return from its commercial break.

"Not presently."

Elizabeth's words twisted through his head like caramel, sticking everywhere. *Weird looks. Sad single ex from a Hallmark movie home from the soulless city, heartsick...*

"Playing the field, huh?" His uncle winked as though Mark was about to break from nearly three decades of stoicism and reveal a hidden flirtatious streak and a phone full of Tinder notifications.

"Our boy doesn't make time for dating," his dad interjected. "Not since Melissa. Carolyn and I will have to co-opt your future grandkids at this rate."

Mark swallowed a groan. He and Melissa had broken up years ago. Of course, Mark had gone on a date since—a handful, even. But he had, admittedly, been busy recently. A PhD. A bookselling job to supplement his stipend and teaching fellowship. A thesis. All so he could pursue a career in academia and everything that went with it. Purpose. Passion. A version of himself he liked.

Of course, none of that meant anything to his dad. Not the scholarships he'd earned during undergrad, not the doctorate degree he'd completed just a month ago. Mark's ambition didn't count—because it didn't look like ambition to his dad.

Would his dad have respected him if he'd pursued dentistry and returned home to join the family practice as he himself once had? Or to teach at the local high school, as Andrew had? If he were the one marrying Melissa Kent, as Andrew was? If he were playing professional hockey on television right now and broke Ray Bourque's record? What would it take?

"Oh, well," his uncle said with an uncomfortable laugh. "Worked out for my son."

"Sure did. Mark let a good one get away," his dad agreed, eyes trained on the screen. He grabbed a potato chip full of onion dip from the coffee table.

Someday, he'd stop letting his dad's offhand comments knock the wind out of him. But not today. Suddenly, it came rushing back to Mark—the first time he'd seen Melissa and Andrew together in town holding hands. Freshman year of college. Winter break. They hadn't broken the news to him yet. He'd arrived home a day earlier than planned, and they'd wanted to tell him in person.

He and Melissa had broken up after high school graduation. If asked, he'd have said they were both too realistic to try to make the distance between their post-secondary schools work. Truthfully, though, Mark had started pushing her away earlier, shutting down rather than discussing his dad's heavy-handed disappointment that he wasn't following his footsteps to dental school. What if she'd agreed with his dad? What if she encouraged Mark to trust his heart, only for him to let her down? Easier to be alone, only accountable to himself.

Hearing the story from his dad, one would think Melissa had cast him aside for his cousin. Andrew the victor and Mark the loser, never mind the truth.

Without planning to, without knowing what he was doing, Mark heard himself say, "I do have a date, actually. For the wedding."

His mom's gaze rocketed up from her e-reader. "You do?"

What had he done? He gave a silent prayer for God's help. What was it James had written in the Bible? To be *slow to speak*? Usually, Mark had no problem following that credo.

Stupid, stupid, stupid.

His father looked at him skeptically. His uncle looked worried. "Does Andrew know about this? I'm happy to hear it, but I could have sworn he said you'd RSVP'd for one."

Mark wished for a Bruins goal to distract his family. Some once-in-a-lifetime hockey play that would wipe the last minute from their minds. This was Elizabeth's doing. Elizabeth and her caramel voice.

"I did," he said. "My date has her own invitation."

Three rapt pairs of eyes bore into him, the television abandoned.

"Who?" his mom asked, scooting to the edge of her seat.

Oh, he was in for it now.

"Elizabeth."

Even though there was only one Elizabeth on the guest list that he knew of, she blinked at him. "Elizabeth Brennan?" As if he might have meant Elizabeth Bennet. As if a Jane Austen heroine were more likely to date him than the former star of every Herons Bay community theater production and their class valedictorian. Oh, that second one had stung back in the day.

"Elizabeth Brennan," he affirmed. Might as well dig himself deeper into this hole now that he'd grabbed the shovel.

"How did that happen?" she asked, nonplussed. "I didn't think the two of you got along when you were kids."

"She lives in New York." Crickets. "We've both grown up."

His dad, somehow, found reason to frown at this; his

uncle to laugh. "Well, how about that? I'll make sure Gina knows for the seating chart."

Oh, good. "Thank you."

"New York must have changed that girl," his dad said, his brow furrowed. "We saw her type in high school."

"Doug," his mom admonished. But she didn't disagree.

"You ask your cousin how he felt about this?" his dad continued.

Mark stared. *Really?* "They broke up years ago."

"Relax, Doug," his uncle said. "My boy hardly has room to object. He'll be glad to hear Mark found someone."

His dad waved him off. "Fair enough, fair enough."

Not a minute later, his dad and uncle were on their feet cheering for a goal, tension forgotten. Of course, *now* the Bruins scored. Sticking a hand into his pocket, Mark felt the edge of the napkin Elizabeth had given him. *Here's hoping the numbers haven't smudged.*

This wasn't forever. Just for now. After the holidays, he'd find a temporary job and figure out his living situation. And Elizabeth would head back to New York after Christmas. No one would expect them to carry on past the holiday.

His mom was peering over her e-reader at him with worry. Mark remained standing stiff as a plank as the game continued on.

"Was the date Elizabeth's idea?" she said quietly to him alone—not that his dad and uncle were likely to hear her softspoken question over the game anyway.

Originally. But Mark had run with it. He shrugged. "It was mutual."

His mom chewed on her lower lip. "I'm glad you're putting yourself out there. Really. I know you've been lonely since moving home."

She didn't need to add *but* for him to hear the implied conjunction. Why was there always a *but* in this house?

"Be careful," she said finally. "That girl was always sunshine. Beautiful, but I don't want you getting burned."

"You don't need to worry about that, Mom. It's just a date."

Besides. He'd never sunburned easily.

Chapter Three

Another cloudless December day in Herons Bay. Elizabeth spent a moment admiring the fake snowflakes dusting the windows of Daisy's Diner. So far, no signs of a truly white Christmas despite the cold weather.

She lingered outside a little longer, contemplating walking into the diner's bustle and requesting a table for one. So far, she hadn't convinced her feet to move one step closer.

Her parents regretted that they hadn't been able to take her out to breakfast at their favorite diner yet this visit, but they owed their guests a homemade spread each morning. Bed-and-breakfast and all. When Elizabeth had tried to help, they'd shooed her away. Literally. Her mom claimed they wanted her to enjoy her vacation, her dad that the kitchen was crowded enough with the two of them, but Elizabeth suspected they just wanted to preserve their routine.

Standing here on the sidewalk, arms wrapped around herself, Elizabeth worried her lower lip. This would always be her home. But did she still have a place here after nearly a decade in New York?

Which left her considering a table for one. Sure, she could call an old friend to meet her for breakfast, but people were busy with their families this time of year. And besides, Melissa and Andrew had been her best friends growing up. She hadn't dared reach out to either of them this week, with their wedding just days away.

"Elle?"

Speaking of…

Elizabeth knew who she would see before she turned around. Strawberry blond locks. Doe eyes. Freckled skin. The only person who ever called her Elle.

"Melissa," she said, reaching out to wrap her childhood friend in an impulsive hug. "Hi!"

Melissa hugged her back. For a second, they were kids again, as close as ever. "I thought that was you! I didn't know you were home yet."

"Just the other day." Once, Melissa would have been her first call upon arriving home.

A moment later, they'd disentangled, the distance between them restored. That was when Elizabeth realized that Melissa hadn't been taking a solitary stroll through town. Next to her stood a familiar man with hair the color of hay and kind eyes she'd once lost herself in. Beside him were his parents.

"Hi, Andrew," she said, wondering whether it would be more awkward to hug her ex-boyfriend or forgo hugging him. Which would say more? She gave a wave to his parents. "Mr. and Mrs. Hayes."

She'd always liked Andrew's parents. Though she hadn't spoken to them much since high school, they smiled at her as though mere days had passed.

"Lovely to see you again, Elizabeth," his mom said.

"Thanks for making it home this week," Andrew said,

making the to-hug-or-not-to-hug decision for her with a quick, friendly arm around her shoulder. "Means a lot to Mel and me."

Elizabeth smiled and nodded. They were getting married a day before Christmas. Where else would she be but home? "Thank you for inviting me."

"We're going to head in and snag a table," Brad Hayes said to his son. To Elizabeth, he said, "We'll be seeing you and Mark at the wedding. Our thanks to your parents for all their work this week!"

By the time Brad and Gina had disappeared into Daisy's, Elizabeth was still blinking. *You and Mark.* Huh? Had someone overheard her conversation with him last night? Or enough of it anyway, to draw the wrong conclusion? He'd made it snow-globe clear he wasn't going anywhere with her.

Melissa rubbed her palms against her arms for warmth, and said, "I can't believe you didn't tell me you and Mark were dating! Don't worry, we fixed up the reception seating chart to keep you two together."

Andrew ran a hand through his light hair. "I almost didn't believe it." A pause. "My parents aren't confused, are they? You're the Elizabeth he's taking to the wedding?"

She didn't know about his parents, but Elizabeth was certainly confused.

Melissa gave Andrew's shoulder a playful swat. "We're not in high school anymore, babe. I'm sure they have plenty in common now."

Andrew squinted his blue eyes and sounded out, "You *have* both lived in New York."

Melissa's laugh tittered, whether from cold or nerves. "There must be more than that."

Improv wasn't Elizabeth's specialty, a fact she'd never lamented more. Blank. Her mind was a total blank.

"I can't wait to hear all about how you two reconnected," Melissa said. "Let's catch up later, okay? Things are hectic with the wedding, but I still need my mocha breaks."

"Yes," Elizabeth said, thankful for the lifeline. That, she knew how to answer. "Please. Anytime. I can't wait to hear about everything."

Melissa and Andrew hustled inside, and Elizabeth wandered away, her table for one forgotten. Had *she* misunderstood Mark yesterday? They'd never communicated very well with each other, but she remembered his no.

Pulling out her phone, she was about to click into Facebook to message him when she saw two new texts from an unknown number.

Typically, Elizabeth would assume spam. But given the timing and the Massachusetts area code.

She paused at a bench to open the messages. Nothing annoyed her parents more than people who walked blindly down the street, eyes glued to their phones, expecting passersby to navigate around them.

I need to talk to you, the text read.

Even if he hadn't immediately followed up with This is Mark, Elizabeth would have put that together for herself. It was either Mark or a very blunt stalker.

I hear you reconsidered, she texted back. Gossip get to you after all?

For a while, she could see him typing. Typing. Typing. Then: Something like that. Have you had breakfast yet?

Daisy's Diner had been around for longer than Mark had been alive. It looked the same as ever: daisy paintings on the walls, blue leather booths filled with families, a counter with swiveling chairs most often occupied by silver-haired men chatting over crab cake eggs Benedict and chorizo hash. And, of course, the specials board that hung behind the counter, its every spare inch covered by the cursive handwriting of Daisy herself. Often, customers needed it decoded, especially as Daisy had gotten older and her penmanship shakier. But no one ever complained.

It was the oldest breakfast spot in town, after all, and Herons Bay was loyal. The best breakfast in town, too, bustling enough that no one would overhear their conversation.

Still…

"I was thinking we'd meet somewhere outside town," Mark said once he'd settled into the booth Elizabeth had snagged for them. Mattapoisett. Fairhaven. New Bedford. Anywhere his cousin, aunt, uncle and ex-girlfriend weren't also eating breakfast. Even though they were seated across the room, he felt their presence like an itch on his back, persistent and unreachable.

Oblivious, Elizabeth raised an eyebrow at him. "Ashamed to be seen with me?"

She was teasing. He could tell by the curve of her lips. Still, Mark felt the need to clarify. "That would pose a problem since I'm apparently taking you to this wedding."

"I heard something about that." Menu open, Elizabeth peered at him over its laminated edge. "From Melissa and Andrew, actually. What changed your mind?"

Mark winced, taking a bitter sip of his black coffee. Truth be told, he preferred it with milk. But dairy didn't sit well in his stomach, and Daisy's didn't carry oat or almond milk.

"This town" was all he said. From what he recalled, Elizabeth and her parents had a charmed relationship. A friendship. Whatever parental tension she'd alluded to last night wouldn't resemble the soul-dimming disappointment in his dad's eyes.

"Herons Bay does feel like a snow globe sometimes."

That was one way of putting it. "For better and worse."

Before he could elaborate or she could reply, Daisy herself strolled over to their table. "Why, Elizabeth Brennan and Mark Hayes. I had to come out and see for myself to believe it."

The diner owner's once dark hair had gone gray long before Mark had left town. But she still wore her hair in the same ponytail, tied back with a Christmas-red bow today.

"Hi, Mrs. Mitchell," Elizabeth said, rising to give her a hug. "So good to see you."

Daisy harrumphed. "You're a grown woman now, so call me Daisy. And don't bury the lede. People count on me to know the local gossip, you know."

Elizabeth laughed. "How could I forget?"

Her good humor seemed so natural. Mark, meanwhile, felt frozen under the magnifying glass. Lecturing hundreds of freshmen on American lit? No problem. A conversation in his hometown diner? Deer in headlights.

"The way the two of you used to bicker back in high school! Who would have guessed you'd be dating now?"

"Neither one of us," Elizabeth said.

Maybe she *did* have more of a sense of humor than he remembered.

"God likes to surprise us sometimes," Daisy said before growing businesslike again. "Now, tell me all about New York. Are you still performing?"

Elizabeth seemed to falter for a second. Mark opened his mouth to say something—who knew what?—to divert the conversation, but she recovered quickly enough.

"I'm still auditioning."

She sounded as cheery as ever. No reason for Mark to suspect that Elizabeth's smile had grown forced.

"Good for you," Daisy returned. "I expect your parents to tell me when you make it on Broadway. Just about the only thing that could get me back to New York at this age." She faced him. "Now, Mark, you finished a doctorate degree this year, is that right?"

He nodded. "Yes, ma'am."

"Congratulations. That's a noble endeavor." The older woman beamed. "But call me Daisy, please. I might have gray in my hair, but I'm still not a ma'am."

It meant more than Mark wanted to admit, hearing those words. *A noble endeavor.* Would it be so hard for his father to echo that sentiment?

"Now, the kitchen will be needing me, but it's lovely to see the two of you. Enjoy your breakfast."

"Lovely to see you, too," Elizabeth said. "You still serve my favorite pancakes in the world."

"You sweet girl." She turned to Mark. "Don't you start bickering with her while I'm gone."

This was the second time she'd used that word, but Mark didn't remember bickering with Elizabeth. Yes, they'd competed as teenagers. And argued. Occasionally. Their double dates had often devolved into debates over whatever book they'd just read for English class, with Melissa and Andrew playing mediators. And they'd often disagreed over what movie to see after they finished their burgers or pizza—she'd always advocated for whatever musical or rom-com was currently play-ing, and he'd routinely voted for literally anything else.

Bickering sounded affectionate. Playful. Friendly.

Mark forced himself back to the present with another bracing sip of coffee.

"That," he whispered across the table, though the diner was far too full of chatter for anyone to overhear them, "is why I was thinking we leave town for breakfast."

"I wasn't the one who told our exes we'd started dat-ing," she pointed out, very calmly. Very rationally. Very reasonably. "You know how gossip spreads here."

Usually, Mark was the calm, rational, reasonable one. Now, he was left to sputter, "This was your idea."

"The wedding date part was my idea." She glanced around and lowered her voice. "But Melissa thinks we were dating in New York. I didn't plan to lie to anyone."

"I didn't, either. My family—they don't always lis-ten." He'd only told them he had a date—not that he and Elizabeth were *dating*. Correcting them now, after they'd spread the supposed news to his extended family, felt too complicated. Too migraine-inducing.

Elizabeth had just opened her mouth to counter when a college-aged waitress with a strip of peppermint-pink in her platinum hair came over to take their order.

"Cranberry apple pancakes, please," Elizabeth said, handing over her menu. "With chocolate chips."

Mark felt dull in contrast, ordering his standard poached eggs and sourdough toast. Same thing he or-dered every time he went out for breakfast, no matter where. Cranberry apple chocolate chip pancakes did sound pretty good right now.

"I think," Elizabeth said once the waitress left, "that I have a solution. For the dishonesty."

He was all ears.

She leaned in. "We have four days until the wedding. As long as we go on a few dates between now and then, we're not exactly *lying.*"

Mark felt himself nodding.

"Though that does require you to—" she lowered her voice again, this time with faux gravity *"—spend time with me."*

He felt a smile kick at the corners of his mouth. "I think I can handle that."

Could *she*? was the question. As anyone in town would say, sweet Elizabeth Brennan was much easier company than taciturn Mark Hayes. And he doubted *taciturn* would be anyone's word of choice. *Grumpy. Cold. Aloof.*

"Good," Elizabeth said, pulling a notebook and pen from her bag. "Now, this can be our second date. We'll call coffee last night the first."

"Pretty bad first date," he tried to joke.

"Believe it or not, I've endured worse. At least you didn't spend the whole time rambling about conspiracy theories or investment banking."

"Dating in New York can be rough," he heard himself reply. Of all the clichés. But it was better than saying something like, *Maybe you're dating the wrong kinds of guys.* As if it were her fault.

She nodded. "Hopefully, this won't be. I think one outing a day should cover it."

Easy enough. One of the several knots of tension he'd been ignoring in his chest unwound. He'd been planning to spend most of the week continuing to search job postings and catching up on pleasure reading, but he dreaded his dad's commentary. At least this would get him out of the house.

"Now," Elizabeth said, "what are your favorite things to do at home?"

She'd written *Date Ideas* at the top of the page, along with the actual date. All with perfect penmanship of course. Some things never changed. She'd carried a journal back in high school, too, and had always been one for lists. How many pro-con lists had he overheard Melissa make with her? She might, he vaguely recalled, even have tried to help him make one back when he'd been debating colleges. Knowing his high school self, he couldn't have been very receptive.

"We could get coffee again," he said. "I'll pay this time. You know, to make up for—" being a jerk? Turning her down just to spring this on her? "—last time."

"Thank you," Elizabeth said. "There's nothing to make up for, though. We can split everything."

He wished she weren't so gracious. So objectively gorgeous, with her golden hair falling into her face as she tapped her pen against the paper. It would make it easier to hold on to his old ambivalence toward her.

"You like books!" she burst out a second later, penning *Book shopping!* into her notebook. "We can go to Blue Heron together."

Mark did love Blue Heron Books. No matter how many bookshops he'd frequented in New York, none of them quite measured up to Blue Heron. He couldn't explain it. He'd been to larger bookstores with wider selections. But none of them felt like home to him.

"Works for me," he said. "I have, uh, some last-minute Christmas shopping to do anyway."

Elizabeth seemed like the type of person who would have her Christmas shopping done by Labor Day, but all she said was, "Perfect. Me too. Plus, I want to start reading more this year. Maybe I'll finally buy a copy of *Ulysses*."

"Please don't," Mark said. "If you're going to read James Joyce, be kind to yourself and pick up anything else."

She raised a brow. "Aren't all you academic types supposed to love ambiguous, pretentious tomes?"

"I'm a rebel," he deadpanned. His brow furrowed as he belatedly processed her saying that she'd start reading more this year. "You were always a reader back in school. Not anymore?"

Elizabeth shrugged. "I still read the news and my Bible every morning. But novels... I guess they were the first to go once life got busier." A beat. "I miss them."

"Busy job?" he asked. This was the sort of thing he should know about a significant other, fake or otherwise.

A nod of her heart-shaped face. "Sort of. I trade a lot of shifts around so I can make open calls and auditions, and I cover for my coworkers when they need the same. It's a little...a lot. Between working and auditioning and rehearsing."

A little a lot. Made sense. "Shifts?"

"Coffee shop," she elaborated. "Nice people. Health insurance."

He could relate to that, working oneself to the bone for a dream most would have forsaken by now. Before he could dwell on their common ground, she was forging on, changing the subject.

"We could go to Sweet Somethings for one of their candy-cane-making demonstrations. I've seen it a million times, but I never get tired of it."

Neither did he. He remembered spending many December evenings at Sweet Somethings growing up. Especially when he needed an escape from the stress of school or his house. Trite as it might sound, he'd felt God's presence in those quiet moments, watching the staff pull candy into canes. Nothing had centered him more.

What centered Elizabeth? "I suppose you'd want to see a show, if we were in New York." If they were really dating.

"I remember your feelings on musicals," she said, matching his levity. "I wouldn't do that to you."

"I don't think anyone would believe I'm dating Elizabeth Brennan if I didn't offer up a night out at the theater."

A brief falter of her smile. "You're more thoughtful than most of the guys I've actually dated, then."

And he wanted to fidget again. What did he say to that? For years Elizabeth Brennan had existed in the back of his brain as the perfect golden girl with the perfect golden life. He didn't want to imagine her on disappointing dates. Or ill-fated auditions, for that matter. He didn't want to see the seams in her smile.

"Kidding," she said, breaking the silence that stretched between them. "Kind of."

He wished he had a first date horror story to trade for her laugh. But he'd have to date more to accumulate those. The few dates he'd gone on since college had been…fine. Awkward small talk. No spark. No stories.

"You're making it hard for me to dislike you," he said honestly.

"Pity for the win," she quipped.

It wasn't pity, though. Something more dangerous beat at his heart—connection.

Out of the corner of his eye, he saw Andrew standing up, along with the rest of his table, already done with breakfast. Somewhere along the line of their conversation, he'd forgotten all about them over there.

His cousin gave him a grin and a goodbye wave before heading out. Melissa raised her free hand as well, the other knotted through Andrew's. She looked thinner than she had at Thanksgiving dinner. Her face gaunter. Wedding preparations must be taking their toll on her. Or maybe that was the lighting.

The door jingled as they left. Meanwhile, Mark and Elizabeth's waitress had returned with their food.

"Oh, my gosh, this is so good," Elizabeth said, already a few bites into her pancakes. "Want some?"

Mark didn't usually allow himself to start his day with sugar. A childhood rule he had never kicked. Still, comfort food was calling to him, and when he saw the joy brightening Elizabeth's green eyes, he couldn't help but nod. "Please."

He gave silent thanks for his food and then vocal thanks for the fluffy strip of pancake she slid onto his plate. It was decadent in his mouth. Addictive. That was the problem with sugar. Once you had a bite, you wanted more.

Elizabeth grinned at him. "What do you think?"

Perfect. Mark stared down at his plate. "A little too sweet for me."

Chapter Four

Elizabeth was curled up on the living room couch with her laptop, searching for upcoming casting calls, when her phone chimed.

Her heart hiccupped in her chest, the way it had at any sign of life from her phone for the past few days. Mary Tyler Morkie perked up at her feet, tilting her head.

"Cross your paws for me," she whispered to her dog. Meanwhile, Elizabeth crossed her fingers. She had set the email she used exclusively for auditions and callbacks to sound with wind chimes at any new messages before coming home. So far, she'd only gotten spam and false starts. But maybe this one…

Elizabeth tapped her inbox, her heart skyrocketing— and promptly plummeting. More spam. No news. She really wanted to perform in this latest play she'd auditioned for, a new show that followed the lives of various women from the Bible.

At least her parents weren't home to witness her disappointment. When she'd returned from Daisy's Diner, they'd asked her to watch the B&B, in case this afternoon's check-in arrived early, while they got supplies for this week's activities. A hot cocoa social. Christmas cookie decorating. Some festive crafts for the kids staying with them.

Everything her parents had always talked about doing if they kept the B&B open for Christmas. *They* were living their dream.

Lately, Elizabeth was starting to wonder if God was telling her to rethink hers. With each rejection, each closed door. In high school and even college, she'd gotten a role in every show she'd auditioned for. Some smaller than others, of course, some in the chorus, but always something. Breadcrumbs to let her know she was on track. More often, though, a whole baguette.

She hadn't gotten a breadcrumb in a while now.

Oh, Elizabeth had known it would be hard. Broadway was *Broadway* for a reason, after all. But she hadn't expected the toll it would take on her spirit. The nagging fear that she was letting down everyone who had ever believed in her, that she wasn't living up to the potential God had given her. That she was, at twenty-eight, a failure.

Elizabeth had only ever wanted to work in theater. To immerse herself in art, to create stories on stage, to make an audience laugh and cry and applaud. Once, she'd felt blessed to have discovered God's purpose for her so young. Now, she doubted.

Okay, she was making herself sad.

You haven't heard back yet. She could still get good news to finally share with her parents this Christmas. God worked all kinds of miracles all the time. Just look at Mark. Last night, he'd shut her down without hesitation when she'd suggested they attend this Friday's wedding together. And now they had a week of fake dates set.

As if sensing her malaise, Mary Tyler Morkie crawled up onto her legs, pawing at her laptop. *Make room for me*, her big brown eyes beseeched.

Elizabeth eagerly accepted the excuse to set her laptop aside. Scrolling and searching for acting opportunities had become a compulsion. What if her big break was out there right now, waiting for her to find it? One role could change everything.

Mary Tyler Morkie pawed at her again, whining a little. *Pay attention to me, please.*

"You're right," Elizabeth said, ruffling her dog's blond bangs. "I'm on vacation. No point in worrying about this now."

No point in worrying at all. It wouldn't change anything. She had to trust that God had a plan for her, that this was all leading somewhere fruitful, that she wasn't failing.

Well, that definitely counts as a worry.

Another chime got her attention—this one from the doorbell rather than her phone. Her dog bolted up to run to the door, ears and legs at attention, barking a greeting at their visitor. The guests her parents were expecting in a few hours were probably here early.

"Quiet, MTM," she hushed.

Elizabeth followed her into the front hall. Customer service smile in place. Key in hand. When she opened the door, however, it wasn't to find a luggage-laden guest.

"Hey, Elle." From beyond the threshold, Melissa gave her a timid wave.

The surprises just kept coming today.

A light blue hat and matching scarf nearly swallowed her freckled face, but Elizabeth would recognize Melissa anywhere. It was like their hug today, muscle memory, despite the holes that time had worn into their old friendship.

Mary Tyler Morkie wagged her tail, running a lap around Melissa's feet.

"Oh, hi!" Melissa said, bending over to pet her dog. "Your parents actually got a dog? After you begged all those years growing up?"

MTM lapped happy kisses onto her new friend's palm.

"She's mine actually," Elizabeth said, scooping her squirming welcome committee of a pup into her arms. "A temporary B&B staff member. Very friendly."

"What a cutie-pie," Melissa cooed to MTM. To Elizabeth, "Good for you. You've always been a dog person."

"I love her a lot."

Mary Tyler Morkie preened, as if she understood the compliment. Maybe she did. Elizabeth's dog seemed to have an ever-expanding grip on the English language— the words *cookie*, *walk* and *fetch*, for instance, she knew well.

It took a minute for Elizabeth to realize that MTM was being a better hostess than she was. Melissa was still standing on the other side of the threshold.

"Oh! Please come in. It's been a while," Elizabeth joked. Sort of joked. When had Melissa last visited her at her parents' house? When had Elizabeth last visited her while home in Herons Bay? A two-way street neither of them had traveled in a long time. "Are you here to see a guest?"

"For you, actually. Any chance you're up for a coffee break?"

Now, what could this be about? Rather than head back into town, Elizabeth ushered Melissa into the dining room.

"It's not the Coastal Café holiday menu," she said of

the coffee and tea station set up for guests, "but I shouldn't leave until my parents get back."

With today's track record of surprises, an unbooked guest or three should be showing up any minute seeking a room.

"This is great," Melissa said, pouring herself some coffee. "I need to cut back on my mocha intake anyway."

"You outgrew hot chocolate?" Elizabeth teased. As a kid, Melissa had carried a thermos of hot chocolate to school every day from late November to mid-March. A plastic bag of marshmallows, too, which they'd often ended up sharing.

"Never. Kind of. Teaching kindergarteners requires a little more caffeine," she said, holding her fingers apart to mime quite a lot of caffeine. "Not to mention all the— well, the wedding planning."

Elizabeth swallowed, though she hadn't taken a sip of her tea. "How has that been?"

"Oh. You know. A lot."

Elizabeth didn't know, was the thing. Aside from a few gushing texts of congratulations exchanged when Melissa had first posted her engagement photos to Instagram, they hadn't talked about this. Hadn't talked at all.

But they'd started growing apart long before the engagement. "I can imagine." No point in reopening old wounds.

Melissa's chestnut brown eyes swept the room as she stirred her coffee. "I'm so glad your parents decided to stay open this Christmas. It's perfect."

"They'll be glad to hear that."

"Our guests love it so far. Jenna and Lucas—Andrew and I met them in college, they would have checked in with a little girl—they said they've never stayed anywhere cozier."

Elizabeth was pretty sure that made Jenna the guest she'd overheard gossiping about her. She pushed her hair behind her ears and replied, "They'll be glad to hear that, too. Cozy has been the goal."

Melissa sipped her coffee. "I remember. Your parents always used to talk about the B&B they'd open someday back when we were kids."

"And here we are now." Elizabeth looked around the dining room. The coffee bar against the wall, the long mahogany table where they currently sat, the gingerbread-person-patterned tablecloth covering it. Mary Tyler Morkie in the corner chewing happily on her favorite toy on a fluffy dog bed.

"It's a little weird seeing your house like this. I mean, I'd heard they redid parts before opening the B&B. But I keep expecting it to look just like it used to."

Only, it didn't. Much like their friendship. "Long time ago now."

"Yeah." Melissa took a deep breath. "A little weird seeing you with Mark, too. How did that happen?"

Exactly the question she'd been dreading. Fortunately, though, she and Mark had come up with an answer for this question at breakfast. Just another script for her to follow.

"We reconnected over the wedding actually." Keep it simple. Keep it true. "Pretty recently."

"I told Andrew that was probably it. That's what I came over to talk to you about—the wedding."

Elizabeth steeled herself to hear whatever had Melissa fidgeting. "Oh?"

A blush burned her cheeks, far redder than her strawberry blonde hair.

"Um. Andrew is suddenly saying that he wants Mark to be a groomsman even though we'd *agreed* we were only doing a best man and maid of honor. Josh, his college roommate, and my sister. He changed his mind when he heard Mark was taking you." Huh? "Something about not asking him before so as not to draw their family's attention to Mark attending stag? I don't entirely get his logic. But I really am so happy for the two of you—"

"Thank you," Elizabeth rushed to intercept her. "I don't want you to get the wrong idea, though. It's really casual." Convenient. Fake. Her turn to blush.

Melissa eyed her skeptically, probably thinking that neither she nor Mark had ever been the casual type. Another reminder that Melissa didn't know her very well anymore. Casual dates were all Elizabeth had the time or will for, currently.

"Even so. Andrew is talking to Mark right now. And Mark isn't going to want to say yes, but he will."

"You don't know that," Elizabeth said even as she suppressed a wince. She hadn't meant to plunge Mark into this front and center.

"You're right. I don't really know Mark anymore. And, don't get me wrong, I hate that he and Andrew have grown apart over the years. It's hard not to feel a little responsible."

Elizabeth shook her head. "If Mark and Andrew have grown apart, that's on them. Don't put that on yourself."

Just as she couldn't blame Andrew for the distance that had sprouted between Melissa and herself. Friendships required work. Intention. Effort. Honesty. And Elizabeth had never managed to tell Melissa how much it had hurt when she and Andrew had started dating. Nor had Melissa ever told her how she and Andrew had fallen in love. Elizabeth had smiled and wished them well; Melissa had sighed her relief and thanked her for understanding. And then they'd each returned to their respective college for the next semester.

And that had been that.

No frank conversations about how recently Elizabeth and Andrew had broken up. No questions about the timing; no risk of uncomfortable answers. Admitting Melissa had hurt her would have made Elizabeth feel like a victim. And she hadn't wanted to play that role, had patched up the holes in her armor with positivity and platitudes to avoid it. No wonder they hadn't managed a real conversation with each other since.

"Thank you," Melissa said, after a sip of her coffee. "I hate remembering how it all came out. We didn't get a chance to tell Mark beforehand, and…I don't know. Things haven't been the same between them since. Hopefully, this helps them reconnect."

Elizabeth gave an encouraging nod.

A deep breath. "The thing is, though, our numbers are off now."

Elizabeth stilled as she caught on. She'd been in enough weddings to know how this worked, how unbalanced the photos would look otherwise, especially with such small bridal and groomsmen parties.

"I know the wedding is days away," Melissa went on. "I know I can't ask you to be a bridesmaid on such short notice. But I'm asking you to be a bridesmaid." She shook her head. "I'm awful."

"You're not awful. And I'm happy to do it. But are you sure there isn't someone else…"

Someone else you'd rather ask, someone else you're closer to now, someone else who would make more sense.

"I could ask someone else. But with you and Mark coming to the wedding together, this feels right. Give or take a—" she faltered, then recovered "—a few things, it would be just like we talked about as kids."

Give or take their partners, to start. Give or take a lot of things.

"I remember," Elizabeth said, almost without meaning to. The dream wedding boards they'd created on Pinterest—set to private, of course, and shared only with each other. Back then, Melissa had fantasized about a summer Cape Cod wedding, with the reception somewhere fairy-tale-lavish, like the Chatham Bars Inn or the Wequassett Resort. Blue hydrangeas galore. Bridesmaid dresses to match. A raw bar before dinner and a lemon cake for dessert.

"I still have that old Pinterest board," Melissa admitted, either reading her mind or her face. "It would be nice to have at least one piece of it in my wedding—you could be my something old. Not that you're old. Obviously. We're the same age." She fidgeted with her mug again. "I'm going to be quiet now and let you think."

Elizabeth might not be old, but their friendship was. Beneath the table, she toyed with one of her bracelets.

"Melissa, I'm honored, but…" She reached for something to say. Did she accept, or did she turn Melissa down? "Is there even time for me to a get a dress?"

Each time she'd been a bridesmaid in the past, she ordered her dress months in advance.

"So, about that," Melissa said. "God provided. My sister's dress—you remember Phoebe?—got lost in the mail, so the site sent her another free of charge." Of course

Elizabeth remembered Phoebe. And they'd always been a similar size. "The original must have been misdelivered or misplaced in some post office sorting room, because it ended up coming a month later. After all that, they just told her to keep both."

That was almost too coincidental to believe. Still, an uneasy wave churned in her stomach. Melissa had better friends than her now, didn't she? More deserving options. More natural options, with whom she wouldn't need to confirm if they remembered her sister.

Something old, she'd called her.

"My mom can make any slight alterations. Not to mention, emerald is one of your colors, so you'll look gorgeous in the photos." A hint of desperation touched her eyes. "Please, Elle?"

This was about convenience and appearances. If Melissa had thoughts of rekindling their friendship, she might have tried to catch up with Elizabeth, ask about her life in New York. But this was a quick fix. Just like her date with Mark. Not romance. Not friendship. And that was fine. Elizabeth hadn't expected more from this week.

Resisting the nervous urge to play with her hair, Elizabeth replied, "How can I say no?"

"See you at the rehearsal dinner, cuz." A hand clapped on Mark's shoulder. A gust of wind as the front door opened.

"Will do," Mark said. Meanwhile, his heart had turned into an anchor, plunging through his chest as he watched Andrew saunter from his parents' house. "See you."

This was what an impulsive tongue got him. Front and center at a family wedding, alongside a fake date. God sure had some sense of humor.

Nope. Scratch that. Mark had no one to blame but himself for this one.

"Very kind of Andrew, asking you to stand up as a groomsman," his dad said once the door thudded shut.

Mark immediately missed the brisk breeze from the driveway. The crackling fireplace spread heat throughout the room and all over Mark's skin. Of course, Andrew had asked him with both his parents present. Of course, his dad had radiated approval. Of course, his mom had teared up. A scene from a storybook—in which Mark felt like a minor character. An object of the protagonist's pity.

"Good man," his dad added.

Mark couldn't disagree.

"And so thoughtful," his mom said. "I know you might have felt awkward if you were going alone. Family gossip and all. But it's all different now that you have a date."

"Though I still don't see why, out of all the girls on the East Coast, you had to pick your cousin's ex-girlfriend. Or why she picked you, for that matter. Eight million other people in New York, aren't there?"

He doubted his dad would appreciate the honest answer: *Well, I was the most convenient of those eight million people.*

Mark was an adult with a doctorate degree and academic publications to his name and was above that kind of surliness. Though who could say whether that would hold true if he didn't find a job this year.

"Andrew and Melissa don't mind," he answered. Flatly. Coolly. Reasonably, he hoped.

Please, Lord, help me find a job soon. The more time he spent living with his parents again, the more he felt himself regressing into teenage tendencies he'd long outgrown. He needed his own place again. His own life.

Since moving home, he felt like he'd locked himself in a phone booth with his mom's worry for his future and his dad's judgment of his choices. Meanwhile, he was trying as hard as he could to keep faith that he hadn't wasted the last ten years of his life.

No pressure there.

Could he blame his parents, though? Uncle Brad and Aunt Gina were planning their son's wedding right now. His parents were hosting their nearly thirty-year-old son as he searched for an academic position that would put his newly earned PhD to use. The same PhD that his dad had never seen any point in him pursuing.

His dad hadn't even supported him earning a bachelor's in English. Too impractical. The PhD had clearly struck him as beyond the pale. To his dad, a teacher was a teacher, no matter how many times Mark tried to explain why he'd opted for this longer route to employment. That he'd enjoyed pursuing his PhD for its own sake. That, when he found an open position in a literature department, he wouldn't only be teaching. He'd be researching, writing, publishing.

His dad never seemed to hear him. Meanwhile, his mom would nod, even as doubt burdened her brow.

Oh, they'd congratulated him upon his graduation, but not the way they'd celebrated Andrew's engagement. No question which accomplishment meant more to them.

Shoving those thoughts away, Mark listened as his dad went on, "As I said. Good man. I wouldn't have had my ex-girlfriend in my wedding."

"Oh, Doug, you're talking like they broke up months ago rather than years. And besides, Melissa could have said the same to him about Mark. By that logic, our son should have said the same to both of them and refused."

An impatient wave of his dad's hand. "That's different."

One would think, at a certain point, his father's off-hand comments would stop slicing him like papercuts. One would think. *Because I couldn't possibly have meant as much to Melissa as Elizabeth meant to Andrew? Because I couldn't possibly feel uncomfortable?* More likely, it was simpler. He just mattered less. To his dad anyway. A real ugly duckling.

The thing about the ugly duckling story that had always bothered him. even after the duckling grew into a swan, he still hadn't fit into his old life. He'd had to make a new one.

Mark would never have refused Andrew's offer. Of course not. Family was family, and one said yes when his cousin asked him to be a groomsman—even if said cousin asked days before the ceremony. Even if said cousin had only asked after one had decided to bring a date. Even if one hadn't felt close to said cousin in a long, long time.

But was it so much to ask that his dad look at things from his perspective for once?

Was it so unreasonable to wish that Andrew had actually talked to him about this? Given him more than a ten-minute drop by the house to share his change of heart? He hadn't wanted a grand gesture from Andrew. Just a real conversation, the kind they'd had as kids before adulthood had filled their time and taken them their separate ways.

"And Mark's happy to do it, isn't that right, son? Might be the closest he comes to getting married himself." His dad laughed at his own joke. His mom gave a pained smile.

Mark cleared his throat. "That's funny."

His dad retorted, "Well, we all know this date with Elizabeth Brennan isn't going anywhere."

"Doug," his mom warned. But she didn't disagree with him. And they weren't wrong. In the far future, once he had tenure and security, maybe he'd pursue a relationship. Until that day, why bother? Love had strings, as his parents kept reminding him, and Mark couldn't bear any more of those just now.

"What?" His dad shrugged. "Even if they were…compatible or whatnot, she lives in New York. And who can say where Mark is off to from here. No news yet?"

Find bruise. Apply pressure. His dad had a knack for that.

"No. Not yet," Mark said. "Usually, interviews continue into the spring. You'll be the first to know."

"Doesn't seem right to spend ten years of your life on a degree and graduate without a job lined up."

Hard to tell if his dad was sympathizing with him or castigating him. The latter seemed the safer bet.

"I'll find something," Mark said, trying to speak faith into fact. "Don't worry. I won't be in your hair long."

"Oh, Mark, that's not what your dad meant." His mom laid a hand on his arm. "We love having you home. It's a blessing, after all those years you spent in New York."

His dad gave a firm nod. "Just want to see you settled. Like I was at your age. Like Andrew is."

Mark tried not to wince. There it was. He prayed for God to clear his heart of the envy piercing his chest. He didn't want to envy his cousin. He *didn't* envy his cousin, didn't want his life. He liked his own. His dad just made it hard to remember that sometimes.

"I better talk to Elizabeth," he heard himself say. "Coordinate."

"I'm sure she's thrilled, too," his mom said.

He managed a nod before opening the front door.

"Don't forget a hat and gloves!"

Overheated as he felt, Mark still obliged. Lifting his coat from the rack with one hand, he grabbed blindly through the basket on the front hall table for a hat and gloves with the other.

"Sure thing, Mom."

Frosty fresh air welcomed him outside. His mind remained staticky. Without letting himself think too much about it, he pulled up his text messages, clicked on his thread with Elizabeth and sent, You feel like taking a walk?

Chapter Five

Mark's text had come through like a lifeline. Unexpected and exactly what Elizabeth had needed. She thanked God for his timing as she walked Mary Tyler Morkie to the local beach, her dog's furiously wagging tail in tempo with her short-legged steps.

The same beach that the residents and visitors of Herons Bay flooded over the summer would be quiet this time of year. No sunbathing or swimming to be done in December. Still, Elizabeth had always appreciated the serenity of a wintertime stroll down the beach. Icy cold or not, the waves were still beautiful, lapping on, never ceasing to strive for land.

It also didn't hurt that the beach allowed dogs to roam its sand from October to May. Mary Tyler Morkie took no time at all to fall in love with the seaside walk.

Elizabeth spotted Mark quickly—the only other person in the pebbled parking lot. His dark hair curled out of a pine green hat with a red pom-pom hanging from it. For such a serious man, he looked almost silly. Incongruously cute. She shook her head. Shook herself. Mark was handsome, that was a fact. But he wasn't cute. Cute led to crushes, which led to dating and labels and love. Neither of them were looking for any of that.

Besides. She didn't even know if he was moving back to New York.

Bad thoughts. New thoughts. Lifting her free hand in greeting, she broke into a light jog to keep up with Mary Tyler Morkie, who had started running at the sight of Mark's tall figure. Like he was a tennis ball she had just thrown in a game of fetch.

"Sweetheart," Elizabeth squeaked. "We don't have to race."

Mary Tyler Morkie did not agree. Had Elizabeth loosened her hold on the leash, her dog would be sprinting. When they reached Mark, MTM started yipping happily, twirling in circles at his feet.

Hi! she seemed to say. *Hi, hi, hi! Are you a friend? Be my friend!*

Mark stared.

Over coffee and breakfast, Elizabeth had found Mark's face unreadable. She was starting to wonder, however, if he suffered from resting grump face—if his strong jaw and sculpted cheekbones, all the angles of his face, gave an unfair impression of coldness. Granted, his Mr. Darcy brooding didn't help, but…

Off track. She had veered off track.

Her point being that often, she had found Mark unreadable, but not right now. Right now, he was staring down at her dog with absolute bafflement.

"What is happening?" he asked.

"She's saying hi."

Mary Tyler Morkie wagged her tail in agreement, doing another twirl.

"And who is she exactly?"

A coincidence that *she* happened to woof again at that exact moment, as if introducing herself. A chatty mix, morkies.

"Mary Tyler Morkie," Elizabeth answered.

"Mary Tyler *what*?"

"Morkie," she repeated as he crouched down to give her a dog a proper hello. "As in a Maltese-Yorkie mix?"

"Named after *The Mary Tyler Moore Show*?"

"Of course." She squinted. "You watch *The Mary Tyler Moore Show*?"

"No. But I remember when you and Melissa went through a '70s phase."

Ah. Her lips curved as she watched Mark give her dog a belly rub—a difficult feat, given the plaid jacket she'd bundled Mary Tyler Morkie's little legs into before braving the chill outside.

"Do you ever call your dog anything other than Mary Tyler Morkie?" he asked.

Elizabeth pretended to think that over, pressing her lips together to keep her amusement from showing. "No."

"Really? Not a single nickname?"

She tilted her head—she *could* tell him that MTM would suffice—before shaking it. "To strangers, she only answers to Mary Tyler Morkie."

"That's…" he trailed off as her dog rolled back onto her stomach and started licking kisses onto his palm. "Pretty cute."

Elizabeth knelt next to him on the gravel, unable to resist giving her dog a few scratches of her own. Did animal love languages exist? Because her dog's had to be physical touch.

Also quality time, actually. And gifts—she liked her treats and toys. Words of affirmation—she enjoyed hearing her praises sung. Not to mention acts of service—she quite appreciated being waited upon. Fine. Mary Tyler Morkie needed all the love languages.

"I figured you for more of a big dog guy," Elizabeth said to Mark, charmed by his continued attentions to her dog.

"I am. This is the smallest dog I've ever seen."

She covered said dog's tiny, perked ears. "She just broke nine pounds. I think my roommates are giving her too many treats while I'm out."

"That is so small, Brennan."

Despite the low temperature, she could feel her cheeks warming. Only Mark had ever called her by her last name. Most people went with Elizabeth. Melissa had long ago co-opted Elle. Her parents sometimes called her Lizzie. But no one except Mark had ever called her Brennan.

"Shall we?" he asked, nodding toward the winter-still beach.

Nodding, she stood to lead her dog forward on their stroll across the parking lot, through the beach grass to the sepia sand, the rhythmic crashing of the waves and the rock jetties leading out to sea. Despite the chill in the salty air, bright sunlight gazed down on them, skipping across the blue water.

Home.

Tail still wagging, Mary Tyler Morkie pranced contentedly between the two of them.

"I've never seen her run at a stranger like that," Elizabeth said. "And you didn't even have a treat for her."

The corners of Mark's mouth turned up. "Should I bring a treat next time?"

"Only if you want her to follow you home."

"I can take that risk." A beat. "How long have you had a dog?"

She heard his real question: *How does an aspiring actress slash barista in New York end up with a lapdog?*

"A couple years. The family I nannied for had a Maltese, who had puppies. They insisted I take one. I fell in love."

"Ah." Another beat. "I can tell."

"Plus, I have roommates who work from home a few days a week, so there's almost always someone there with her while I'm out."

They carried on a few more steps in silence before she spoke again, unable to ignore the elephant on the beach. "I was surprised to get your text."

"We did include a walk on the beach on our list," he replied carefully.

"I was thankful for your text," she clarified. "I'm guessing you've just seen Andrew?"

He kept his gaze fixed ahead of them. "I'm guessing you had just seen Melissa. Good conversation?"

"Well, I'm a bridesmaid."

He smiled grimly. "I'm a groomsman. That doesn't answer the question."

Elizabeth was tempted to give an automatic yes, like she had to her parents when they'd asked her the same question. To keep things simple. Worry-shell smooth. But if anyone would understand…

"I don't know if it was a real conversation," she admitted. "I'm not sure when the last time we had a real conversation was."

"Years ago for Andrew and me," Mark said. He didn't murmur the words with self-pity or resentment. Just sober fact.

"Because...because of Melissa?" Elizabeth asked. Should she be asking that? It was too late to turn back.

Another readable emotion from Mark. Two in one day. Once again, that emotion appeared to be sheer confusion. It made his eyes—as deep a blue as the ocean before them—wider, his sharp face softer. "I have no idea."

She could relate to that.

"I don't know what happened between Melissa and me, either," she admitted. "I mean, it definitely started when she and Andrew went public. We told each other everything when we were younger. But all of a sudden, she was too afraid of hurting my feelings to share much about her life when so much of it involved Andrew. And, honestly, I was too afraid of her pity or guilt to tell her how hard that breakup was for me. That whole season of my life."

The loneliness during that first year away from home when she had desperately missed Herons Bay.

She gave a self-conscious shrug and continued, "Somewhere along the way, we stopped talking about all the other important things, too."

Say what one would about Mark, anyone had to give him credit for one thing: he truly listened when someone else spoke. Even when they were kids and she'd found those silences more intimidating than inviting, she had still noticed that. He kept his gaze on her now, visibly digesting what she was saying. Not jumping in to offer immediate advice or judgment or consolation. Simply allowing her to feel.

How surprisingly, sadly rare it was to find someone willing to listen like that. Even those with the best intentions, like her mom, would have been quick to jump in with something like, *Melissa is your oldest friend, sweetie. Just let her know how you're feeling. You'll work things out.* Meanwhile, her roommate Tara, who had seen Elizabeth through that awful winter of freshman year, would insist Elizabeth didn't owe Melissa anything.

Kindly meant. But nothing was that simple. She'd learned to keep this particular topic to her prayers.

"I wish I had known," Mark said. His reply felt sudden to her, out of nowhere, but only because she'd wandered so far into thought. "That winter wasn't an easy time for me, either."

The raw honesty in his voice, the vulnerability she knew he didn't reveal often, almost stopped her midstep. "I thought about reaching out. We were both in New York... I almost did, once. But I wasn't sure how you'd take it."

"Probably not well at the time," he admitted. "I was struggling, and I had it in my head you were above that. Perfect Elizabeth."

"Oh, please, you thought I was annoying," she teased. Sort of teased. Had he really been that unable to see beneath the confidence she worked so hard to project?

"Yes. Because you were always so perfect. Perfect smile, perfect family, perfect grades, perfect plan for your life, perfect words for every occasion. Everyone loved you."

Perfect plan for your life. Elizabeth withheld a wince. Not exactly. Meanwhile, her dog—oblivious to the worries weighing on her soul—tugged impatiently forward. Reaching into her pocket, Elizabeth threw a small tennis ball down the beach and released the leash. Yipping a battle cry, Mary Tyler Morkie went darting after it.

"You had perfect grades, too," she pointed out rather

than dwelling on that point of searing insecurity. "And didn't you break some record on the cross-country team?"

"Almost perfect grades. You beat me for valedictorian, remember?"

Elizabeth didn't like to roll her eyes but couldn't help it now. "*Barely.* You got into every college you applied to. With scholarships!"

Even so, she remembered that no one had ever called him *perfect.* Instead, people had joked about his brooding bookishness. The few times she and Melissa had joined the extended Hayes family for dinner, his own dad would kid that Andrew and Mark must have gotten switched as infants. Awkward jokes—it wasn't really funny, insinuating that Mark wasn't his real son, was it? But she'd assumed them harmless at the time. Some kind of inside family joke she didn't understand.

Now, Elizabeth realized she had no idea what his family truly looked like. Were they close like hers? She and Mark were both only children. For Elizabeth, that meant a tight bond with her parents. She recalled the way Mark would freeze when his dad joked around at his expense. How he'd tensed the night before, when she'd mentioned parental expectations. Somehow, she doubted his family had the same dynamic as her own.

Her dog returned with the tennis ball in her mouth and a happy wag to her tail. She gave a victory twirl before letting Elizabeth throw the ball again.

"I've been blessed with a lot of love," Elizabeth said. "But I was never perfect. Not that I didn't try."

Not that she wasn't still trying. Elizabeth kicked the toe of her shoe through the sand, careful to avoid crushing the shells strewn across it, and continued, "As if I could make sure everything in my life would go according to plan, as long as I had the perfect grades and extra-curriculars and everything else. I was so proud without even realizing it. I wish I'd learned back then to live in the moment and trust God's will to unfold."

Maybe if she had, everything would be easier to handle now. The fear that she would never make it as an actress. The anxiety that accompanied the wait for callbacks and casting decisions. The fear that nibbled away at her day by day. *Please. Please, Heavenly Father, please.*

Elizabeth wasn't sure what she was praying for. Success? Relief? Rejuvenation? Rest? What was God's will for her? His plan? She used to think she knew...

"I wish I'd known a lot of things back then," Mark said. "But we were kids. I don't think we have to keep feeling guilty over some pride, some envy. As long as we don't surrender to it. As long as we keep looking to God."

Was that what he had struggled with? Envy? Of Andrew? Questions rose to her tongue, but she swallowed them. If he wanted to say more, he would.

So, instead, with faux solemnity, she said, "You're the professor. I guess you know what you're talking about."

A corner of his mouth hitched up. "I try." He was utterly distracting for a moment. Charming. Was this what he was like in his element, in a classroom?

Elizabeth looked away and allowed silence to stretch its arms between them for a moment. No, not silence, not really. The crash of the waves. The squawk of the remaining seagulls. The sounds of Herons Bay. Also, the patter of Mary Tyler Morkie's paws across the sand as she ran back to them, tennis ball retrieved.

"How about you?" she asked finally, picking her dog's ball and leash back up. "How was your conversation with Andrew?"

Blinds seemed to fall across Mark's face, any openness obscured. "Not much of a conversation, either."

Oh.

Mark shrugged. "My parents were touched. Maybe I should be, too."

"Melissa said Andrew really wanted you to be in the wedding," she said softly. "It's the only reason she asked me—to balance the numbers."

Thought weighed on Mark's brow. Elizabeth held her tongue, extending him the same courtesy he'd given her. Time to think. Time to gather feeling into words.

"I like my life," Mark said finally. "I've worked hard for it. But I come back here, move in with my parents again and it's like none of it matters. I meant what I said last night—I don't care what most people think of me. But Andrew is different." An exhale. "It's as if he only asked me to be in the wedding once he could give our family proof that I've 'moved on' romantically. From my high school girlfriend. It's ridiculous, not to mention insulting. I thought…" A shrug. A prematurely ended sentence.

Elizabeth could guess what he didn't say—*I thought he understood me.*

"I don't know him well enough anymore to say what he was thinking," Mark finished, resignation lancing his words. "But he should have asked me to be in his wedding from the start if he wanted me as a groomsman. If it mattered to him. It shouldn't have taken a fake date to make it happen."

The cold sea breeze played with Elizabeth's hair; she pushed it behind her ears. "Andrew was never good at that. He likes the grand gestures and sweeping heroics. Not so much the difficult discussions. It's part of the reason we broke up."

To be franker, at eighteen, it was part of the reason he and Elizabeth had imploded. When distance had strained their relationship freshman year of college, it had never culminated in a fight. He wouldn't let it. He insisted on acting as though everything was fine, as though they were still a super couple, until they weren't. Until it was too late.

"Your cousin isn't perfect," she said. "No one is."

A long smooth shell caught her attention as she continued prodding the sand with her foot. Much to Mary Tyler Morkie's disgruntlement—she'd been tugging at the leash again, this time to chase a seagull—Elizabeth paused to collect it.

A worry shell, tossed and polished by the sea. Perfect for stroking as you contemplated or prayed. MTM sniffed it before deciding it was less interesting than some nearby seaweed.

Without thinking too much about it, Elizabeth straightened and set the shell in Mark's gloved, unsuspecting palm. His fingers closed around it on instinct, grazing hers. It came to her a second later, why she'd done it—mind catching up to instinct.

"I always used to carry one of these in my pocket, back in high school," Mark said. The ridiculous, charming pom-pom on his hat bobbed in the wind, but she couldn't focus on that. Couldn't see past his solemn, surprised face.

"I remember."

She hadn't a moment ago. But she did now. All those times stress would crease his brow in study hall, and he'd pull a shell from his pocket to worry with his thumb.

"Thanks, Brennan." Mark gave her a smile—just a small curve of his lips, but it warmed his eyes. She told herself she didn't feel that warmth in her chest. In her heart.

Chapter Six

Dusk had fallen by the time they left the beach. It surprised Mark how quickly evening had crept up on them. How soon their walk winded down.

Other things he hadn't been expecting out of the afternoon: to talk, willingly, about his emotions with another person, the attentions of a Maltese-Yorkie mix named after a seventies sitcom actress and Elizabeth Brennan.

She was still walking at his side, rubbing her palms together, hurrying toward the heated sanctuary of her family's B&B. Mark hadn't planned to walk her home—her parents lived in the opposite direction from his—but he wasn't ready for the evening to end yet. Wasn't ready to face his own home. The choice between barbed small talk with his dad or a retreat to his childhood bedroom seemed too monotonous after a month under his parents' roof.

Too lonely, a quiet voice added to the margins of his thoughts.

Mark clenched his jaw. He'd gone years without getting lonely, despite his limited social circle in the city. He had friends from his PhD program, sure, but an element of academic competition always hovered over any attempts at true intimacy—for funding, for employment, for success. Solitude hadn't bothered him until recently. Trust his hometown to mess with his mind.

"Too—" Elizabeth shivered or sniffled "—cold."

A walk on the beach might have been ambitious for a winter afternoon, he'd admit. It was always colder, breezier by the ocean. But Mark appreciated the winter quiet of their local beach. The seaside serenity that transcended seasons.

Turning onto Water Street, he eyed Elizabeth's puffy pink coat. It looked warm enough, but not nearly as insulated as his own, bought from an outdoors store rather than a boutique.

"Do you want to switch coats?"

A burst of laughter chattered from between her teeth.

"I'm serious," he persisted, beginning to shrug out of his coat. He was bigger. He had more body heat, could sacrifice the down lining for a few blocks.

"Stop," she said. "Please. You're not wearing a woman's puffer jacket."

He raised an eyebrow as they kept up their chilly pace, led by her ridiculously small dog, who didn't seem to know the meaning of the word *fatigue*.

"Why not?"

"Because I'm at least a half a foot shorter than you. For one."

"I hear the cropped look is in," he deadpanned.

She laughed again.

"You're freezing," he tried again. "I'm not. I have a warmer coat. I'm being logical."

She sped up their pace, dragged ahead by the persistent tugging of Mary Tyler Morkie. What kind of dog had a three-word name anyway? The animal whined as if encouraging them to hurry up. One with a big personality apparently.

"You're sweet," Elizabeth said. "But I'm pretty tough."

He was fairly sure she had that backward. Very few people had ever called him sweet before. And he couldn't imagine anyone calling Elizabeth, all softness and smiles, tough.

"Emotionally," she specified. "I'm emotionally tough."

"Well, I can't argue with that." It took a strong spirit to pursue a dream—especially a competitive, cutthroat one like Broadway. Most people didn't make it, but more people didn't try to begin with.

Oblivious to his thoughts, Elizabeth led him onto her parents' street. He hadn't visited their B&B yet, but he had no problem identifying it even before he saw the sign. Colored lights twinkled from their house like so many gumdrops, red and green and blue and yellow and purple. A cranberry wreath hung on the front door, as well as on each candlelit first-floor window, along with copious garlands and red bows. Just as telling were all the cars that filled the driveway.

"Full house, huh?" he asked.

"Just about. It won't be a quiet Christmas." Before they could begin up her driveway, she paused. Deflated. "I forgot. Shoot. My parents are having their hot cocoa social tonight."

"Hot cocoa social," Mark repeated.

"So all the guests can get to know each other," she explained. "I would make your escape now. If you walk me in, they'll definitely want you to stay."

He considered her house. He considered his parents'.

"Unless…you want to stay?" Hope lifted her voice. "You're obviously welcome to."

Want wasn't quite the word. Mark didn't want to meet her parents' guests—wedding guests, he'd assume, who were likely out-of-towners and unknown to him. He didn't want to make small talk with strangers or evade Mr. and Mrs. Brennan's questions about his so-called romance with Elizabeth.

But she seemed to want him. To stay, that was.

"I could use a chance to warm up," he said finally. Even though he doubted dairy-free hot chocolate would feature on the menu. Tea, maybe. Otherwise, he could always cheat and chance an upset stomach.

Much to Mary Tyler Morkie's impatient relief, they started up the long driveway. Every step he took reminded him of just how out-of-character this was for him. Sure, he didn't feel like going home, but he could have taken one of his evening drives. Just him, his car and the passing Christmas lights.

Instead, Elizabeth opened her parents' front door, revealing a living room full of mingling guests and the sounds of the Carpenters' *Christmas Collection*. He recognized it from his parent's rotation of holiday albums. *Rejoice, rejoice*, indeed.

"Don't leave me alone," he said under his breath.

"Ditto," she whispered back, unfastening her dog's leash. Quickly, she gathered the morkie into her arms before she could go tearing through the room, presumably to greet each guest.

Coats on the rack. Hat off before anyone else could see him in the monstrosity he'd pulled at random from his parents' assortment of winter wear.

Elizabeth left the entryway for the living room first, braving the party before he did. No surprise there. Each couple in the room turned to look at them. Of that cluster, Mark only recognized Mr. and Mrs. Brennan. The former had Elizabeth's kind green eyes, the latter her honey-blond hair and bright smile. What similarities did outsiders see between him and his family? Between him and his father?

A stern brow? Cold eyes?

"Elizabeth!" her mom greeted from the center of the gathering, a festive mug in hand. "Come in, come in! Is that Mark with you?"

Every pair of eyes in the room turned on him.

Mark managed a smile. A stilted wave. "Evening, Mr. and Mrs. Brennan. Hope you have room for one more."

His hosts walked over so as not to continue shouting across the room. Mrs. Brennan wrapped her arms around him in a quick hug. "It's wonderful to see you. I'm so glad you and Lizzie reconnected for the wedding. Always seemed a shame you lost touch."

He chanced a look over her shoulder to Elizabeth. Had they ever been in touch? She shrugged.

"Oh, don't look like that," Mrs. Brennan admonished midstep. "Rivals or not, you were friends back in school. The four of you did everything together."

Only because of Melissa and Andrew. Strange that he and Elizabeth never connected in all that time. That he had never seen past her shiny surface. They'd bonded more in the last couple hours than they had in all the years they'd spent together as teens.

Her father took his hand, clasping it in a jovial handshake. "I always meant to thank you, back in the day. Nothing motivated our daughter to study like competing with you. And now you're taking her to this wedding! You have our gratitude."

It was hard to tell with the cold tinging her cheeks,

but he could swear that made Elizabeth blush. "Ignore him," she stage-whispered. "He's high on sugar."

All Mark said was, "The same was true for me, sir." So, he hadn't bonded with Elizabeth growing up. She'd still motivated him. Infuriated him. Inspired him.

"It's a shame you aren't moving back to New York," her mom added. "I hate imagining Lizzie all alone in that big city. We worry about her. It would be nice to know she had a face from home there."

Mrs. Brennan was kind as can be—she couldn't know she'd poked at an insecurity. The reminder that he no longer lived in New York. The uncertainty over where he'd be working, where he'd be living in the future. How long it might take for him to find a position. To be chosen. It was sobering—he needed to remember that everything in his life right now was temporary. He had to get through Christmas and focus on making moves that were more permanent.

"Mom, you know I'm not alone." Now Elizabeth was definitely blushing. Had her mom pushed a button of hers, too? "I have two roommates."

Mrs. Brennan waved that off. "Oh, it's not the same."

Elizabeth's face fell a bit. Only a fraction. Barely noticeable. Mark bristled nonetheless, even though her mom had clearly spoken with affection rather than his dad's judgment. It still hit too close to home.

Then Elizabeth rebounded with a smile and said, "I guess to a B&B owner, an apartment of three *would* sound lonely."

"Touché, touché. I'll stop embarrassing you two," Mrs. Brennan said, leading them over to the refreshment table. "I'm sure you promised Mark some hot chocolate."

No forgetting the Christmas season in here. Even the

napkins they'd set out had gingerbread people waltzing across them. The mugs, either bought specially for the social or saved from previous years, bore illustrations of candy canes and snowflakes and reindeer.

"Now," Mrs. Brennan said, gesturing with flourish to a duo of hot beverage dispensers. "We have your classic hot chocolate and, thanks to our lovely daughter, a dairy-free alternative. Both made with Sweet Somethings chocolate. Take your pick."

"Lizzie insisted on the dairy-free for me," Mr. Brennan confided with a wry grin. "Knew I'd sneak the dairy otherwise, never mind allergies."

"I still think it's just as good with oat milk," Elizabeth replied, as if they'd had this same conversation before. "And besides, you get dairy-free guests."

"I'm not arguing," her dad said, raising his hands in surrender. "Just stating the facts. Which will it be, Mark?"

He scratched the back of his neck. "Dairy-free, please." In explanation, he said, "Lactose intolerant."

Mr. Brennan gave him a shoulder nudge of solidarity. "We appear to be the only two."

Passing Mary Tyler Morkie to her mom in exchange for a mug, Elizabeth said, "I'll join you. As long as I'm not stealing from a guest who needs it."

"The classic is the clear winner so far," Mrs. Brennan declared, stroking her daughter's dog. "Pour away, my dear."

Elizabeth knew her dairy-free alternatives, he'd give her that. Hot chocolate always came out better with oat milk than almond or coconut. Less watery. This was no exception.

"This is great," Mark said to his hosts.

Out of the corner of his eye, he saw his fake date adding a veritable mountain of marshmallows to her mug. He quirked an eyebrow at her.

"They're my favorite part," she said.

Mark considered himself a purist but scattered a few in his own drink.

"Thank you," she said, with an appreciative nod to his efforts.

"I try." The lighthearted reply felt truer than he'd intended. When was the last time he'd *tried* like this in Herons Bay? Joined its community rather than retreat from it? Mark took a quick too-hot sip from his mug.

"Let's get the two of you acquainted with everyone," Mrs. Brennan said. The dog seemed quite content in her arms.

Mark, on the other hand, suddenly felt very warm. He prayed for help. Contrary to popular belief, he didn't consider himself antisocial—more selectively social. He preferred real conversations, real connections to small talk, and those were hard to find with strangers. His social anxiety didn't help matters.

"Lizzie, I think you checked in Jenna and Lucas when they arrived. And their daughter, Isabelle, of course. These two are college friends of Melissa and Andrew's."

"Charmed," Jenna said, her high chestnut ponytail bobbing as she turned to them. "Again."

"Now, we've got to check on the snickerdoodles in the oven, but we'll be back soon. Enjoy the hot chocolate!" Her parents headed for the kitchen.

Elizabeth offered a bright smile and a "Hello again" to the couple. Just a day ago, Mark might not have caught the stilts beneath her cheer, or the way her face turned genuine when she greeted Isabelle. "Hi there! I love your dress."

Mark wasn't good with kids' ages. Isabelle could be anywhere from three to six, for all he knew. However old she was, the curly haired girl spun a little, grinning as the skirt of her red dress flared. "It's a twirly dress."

"That it is. And that bow on the back is so pretty!" Elizabeth said. "Will you show me again?"

Isabelle happily obliged, giving another twirl.

"It's supposed to be for the wedding," Jenna admitted, "but she refused to wear anything else tonight. We're lucky your parents offered up their washer and dryer."

"I know how that goes," Elizabeth said with a small laugh. If Mark hadn't caught her discomfort a moment ago, if she hadn't felt the need to ask him to the wedding, he'd never guess at it now. Would never know he wasn't alone in his.

"Do you have kids?" Lucas asked politely.

"Oh, no," she said. "But I was a nanny for two girls up until recently. One of them went through a phase where she refused to wear anything but dresses for months."

"Sweet," Jenna commented. "Melissa mentioned something about a high school friend nannying. In New York, is that right?"

Elizabeth nodded. "Where are you two from?"

Mark found a brief respite as they chatted about Portland, Maine—until Jenna turned upon him. "What do you do, Mark?"

"I just graduated with a PhD in English literature."

"An academic. Melissa mentioned that, too." She looked back to Elizabeth. "What brought you to New York? There must be nannying jobs here in New England."

"I'm an aspiring actress actually," Elizabeth said, her smile dimming a notch. "Nannying just paid the bills."

"I can't imagine hiring someone to look after my kids," Jenna said with a laugh. "Can you, hon?"

Lucas blinked at his wife. He'd been pouring himself another cup of hot chocolate, stirring it with a candy cane. "No?"

"No. Izzy is far too precious to leave with a stranger." The woman's eyes narrowed slightly. "You never know who you can trust."

Mark narrowed his own eyes at the woman's passive-aggressiveness. But he couldn't guess why this college friend of the happy couple was aiming it at Elizabeth.

Their daughter chose that moment to enter the conversation, tugging on Elizabeth's sleeve and saying with great determination, "I want to be an actress. In Disney movies."

The kid had good timing, he'd give her that. Immediately, the tension eased.

"I think you'll be an awesome actress," Elizabeth said, crouching down to meet her at eye level. "Will you sign an autograph for me? I bet I can get a fortune for it when you're famous."

Isabelle jumped, her dress swishing with the movement. "Can I, Mommy? Please!"

Jenna's sharp eyes softened at her daughter's clear enthusiasm. "Of course. Let me grab a napkin…"

Mark offered up a pen from his pocket. A moment later, Elizabeth was accepting a napkin with a scribbled name on it.

"Thank you, Isabelle," she said. "This is the coolest Christmas present."

Isabelle beamed. Then more shyly said, "Can I have *your* autograph? I've never met a real actress before."

Color overtook Elizabeth's cheeks. "I'm not sure I'm a real actress yet…"

Growing up, Mark had thought he wanted to see Elizabeth Brennan falter from her pedestal. No longer. Now he wanted the relentlessly—annoyingly—optimistic girl he remembered from high school to return. To beam that leading-lady smile, to radiate that old confidence. He opened his mouth to say…something.

But Jenna was already handing her another napkin. "Please."

He watched as Elizabeth swirled her signature between the gingerbread illustrations. "Thank you," she said again, giving it to the girl.

"Thank you!" Isabelle cheered back. An Elizabeth in miniature. Then she lit up at the sight of another kid coming into the room with his parents. "Can I go play with Henry, Mommy?"

Jenna smoothed her daughter's hair and dress before sending her on her way.

"That was kind of you," she said to Elizabeth.

"She seems like a sweet kid," Elizabeth said, looking after the little girl with a fond smile.

"You should have seen her when we tried to convince her to wear another dress," Lucas joked.

With her daughter away at play, Jenna's smile turned strained again. "She's decisive, Luke. That's a good thing."

"Takes after her mother," her husband teased.

She shot him a look that didn't look entirely playful. "You'll give them the wrong idea."

"Shutting my mouth," he said good-naturedly, miming a lock on his lips.

"Now, you'll really give them the wrong idea," she

said with shake of her head, a slash of her ponytail. Then she turned her shrewd look back upon him and Elizabeth. "Forgive my curiosity, but I have to ask—we met Melissa and Andrew freshman year—you're their high school exes, aren't you? We heard so much, back when they got together."

Mark tensed but found a stiff nod for her question. Reminded himself that he would have to face these sorts of questions at the wedding anyhow. Still, his eyes landed on the door.

"Way back when," Elizabeth said. Performer's smile again.

"And you don't feel strange?" she asked, leaning forward, lowering her voice, as if they might disclose their deepest secrets. "Coming to their wedding?"

Mark blinked. "I'm Andrew's cousin. If I skipped his wedding because Melissa and I dated as teenagers, I'd have some explaining to do."

Jenna processed that with a sharp nod—was this woman a reporter?—and then looked to Elizabeth again. "And how about you?"

"I was invited," Elizabeth said, lifting one shoulder. "So here I am."

"I would feel strange," Jenna said. "You don't know me, but I heard *all* about the drama when Melissa and Andrew got together. It sounded like a soap opera."

"It wasn't," Mark said. They'd been young, and they'd all grown up since then.

Elizabeth took a long sip of her hot cocoa. When she finished: "By the time Melissa and Andrew started dating, they were single. Not much of a soap opera. Besides. It was a long time ago."

"You never forget your first love," Jenna persisted, even as her husband shifted uncomfortably.

"Thanks, hon," Lucas said with an unconvincing laugh.

"Oh, you know what I mean."

Though she had been holding up remarkably well under the interrogation, Elizabeth froze now. Smile stuck on her face. Blankness in her eyes. No response coming to her tongue.

Before he could second-guess the impulse, Mark wrapped an arm around her shoulder. Soothed a palm up and down her tense arm.

"The four of us have moved on," he said, slipping into his lecture voice. Cool. Authoritative.

Jenna's eyes bugged. "You two are dating?" Color came belatedly to her cheeks, as if it only occurred to her now how nosy she was being. A sip from her mug. "How lovely."

"We think so," Elizabeth said, relaxing into Mark's touch. Softness assaulted him: her fleece sweater beneath his palm, her honey hair brushing his cheek, the gentle lean of her against him.

Not real, he reminded himself. *This is not real.*

Once again, Jenna and Lucas's daughter had good timing—she came rushing over to tug on Elizabeth's sleeve just then. In a breath, Elizabeth pulled away from him to crouch to her level. Absurd how acutely he felt her absence. It wasn't as though she belonged there. Tucked in his arms.

"Hi," Isabelle said, very seriously. "I want Henry to put on a play with me. Will you help?"

"Right now, hon?" Lucas asked. "It's getting close to your bedtime."

"A quick play!" Isabelle persisted, widening her big brown eyes. "Please, Daddy?"

He looked to his wife, who shrugged. Then to Elizabeth. "If you don't mind…"

Mark's heart sank. He couldn't begrudge her deciding to encourage a little kid, but he didn't particularly want to mingle without her, either.

"I'm happy to!" Elizabeth said, taking Isabelle by the hand. The other, she offered to him. "Will you join our audience, Mark?"

He curled his fingers through hers, thankful for the save.

"Will you?" Isabelle asked delightedly. "And Mommy and Daddy?"

"Tell us when it's ready," Jenna said. "And we'll be there. But it has to be a quick show."

"No problem," Elizabeth said. "Come on, Isabelle, we better get started."

Mark followed, his hand unspooling from Elizabeth's, as she led the girl to the fringes of the living room, where a little boy waited. Without meaning to, Mark shoved his fingers into his jeans' pocket. They still tingled from her touch.

As Elizabeth introduced herself to Henry, Mark gave a wave to the little boy. He got a shy smile in return.

"I told Izzy," Henry said quietly, "I don't know how to put on a play."

"That's okay!" Elizabeth said. "No one does before they do it."

Henry looked unconvinced.

"Yeah, Henry," Isabelle said, a hand on her hip. "You just need to do it."

"We don't have a *script*," Henry countered, brow drawn, dark eyes serious. "Or costumes. Or a stage."

"Well, plays are all about pretending," Elizabeth said. "Can you play pretend, Henry?"

The little boy looked thoughtful. Then he nodded.

"So, we're going to pretend that we have costumes and a stage. And as for the script…" Mark leaned against the wall, watching as Elizabeth explained the concept of improvisation to the two kids. Isabelle latched on immediately. Henry took a little more convincing.

Throughout it all, Elizabeth looked in her element. Eyes bright. Gestures joyful. No doubt that she still loved theater as much as she had growing up. No doubt that she had a gift with kids, either.

Mark's heart panged when Elizabeth turned around to check on him with a small smile.

Not real. Not real.

After Elizabeth directed Isabelle and Henry's makeshift play, after everyone applauded and finished their cocoa and cookies, the living room cleared. Guests were back in their rooms. Quiet now, save for the clutter of abandoned mugs and dessert plates.

Still, Mark remained. To help Elizabeth clean up. To be polite. No other reason.

She had insisted her parents retire for the night, after all. He didn't want to leave her alone to gather all the mugs, to hand-wash and dry them. Even as she repeated, "Mark, you can really go home. I didn't invite you so that I'd have help on cleanup duty. You've done more than enough."

Wielding a dish towel, Mark dried a mug that she'd

just finished lathering. "Stop trying to get rid of me, Brennan. Take the help."

She shook her head with a smile. "Fine. Thank you. For everything tonight. I know it was…"

There were any number of ways she could choose to end that sentence. Probably all true, too. But Mark left it at, "Good practice for the wedding."

"Right." She scrubbed at the rim of a cocoa-stained mug.

"And good hot chocolate."

Good company. He didn't say that aloud. He couldn't say that aloud. She'd know he meant hers.

"My parents will be glad to hear it," she said, smiling at him.

As they settled into a routine, a handoff of washing and drying, Mark focused on the sound of the faucet. The swipe of the sponge. The hummed Christmas song hiding under Elizabeth's breath. Then her soap-damp fingers brushed his at the next mug swap, and it all blurred.

Mark cleared his throat. "Didn't expect to see a show tonight."

A quiet laugh. "Thank you for putting up with that. I couldn't say no."

"You were really good with them."

Elizabeth cleaned busily. He'd just started to doubt whether she'd answer at all when she said, "It was good for me. I know it was silly and quick and just for fun. But it's been a long time since anything about theater has been fun." A beat. "You know, I think I was around Isabelle's age when I decided I wanted to act. My parents took me to see my first live musical, and I came home shrieking all the songs. When they finally signed me up for my first community theater show, I fell in love with it. Declared I'd be on Broadway, someday, before I really understood what Broadway was. It's been a longer journey than I expected."

"You're not even thirty yet. I think you've got time." God's timing wasn't theirs. She didn't need him reminding her of that.

Elizabeth stared down into the sink again, scrubbing intently, lost in thought once more.

"Maybe," she said belatedly. Wistfulness colored her voice; she shook her head. "But enough about me. When did you decide to get a PhD?"

"Well, I didn't know at age four."

"You've always carried a book everywhere, though. For as long as I've known you anyway."

It struck Mark that Elizabeth had known him for a very long time. Even if they'd never connected as kids, never really gotten to know each other, she'd met him back in elementary school. He remembered her back then, too—perfect pigtails, her arm pin-straight in the air for every question from their teacher. What did she recall about him? A boy hiding in the corner with a book? A shadow of his star cousin?

"You're right. I've always been a reader. Growing up—well, I needed the escape. But studying literature didn't seem like a real option to me back then. My parents expected something more practical," Mark said, keeping his eyes on the mug he was meticulously drying. "My scholarship meant I could study what I wanted, though, without their input. And the more literature courses I took, the more I admired the English professors at my university. The way they could mine new meanings from centuries-old texts, the passion they had for their specialties, the enthusiasm the good ones could inspire in their students. By senior year, I knew I wanted to stay in academia. Become one of them."

God willing.

"It hasn't been an easy road," he continued. "But I know it's what I'm supposed to be doing."

Elizabeth sniffed. Finally, he forced himself to set the mug down with other dry drinkware. To accept another from her. To look at her.

She met his glance with glossy eyes. A wavering smile.

"You tearing up on me, Brennan?"

"Of course not," she said, voice a little wobbly. "I just— It's a good reminder. That God always has a plan, even if we can't see it from the start. I needed to hear that."

"Sap," Mark said softly, even though he'd thought the same before.

"Yeah," Elizabeth said. "Duh. Theater kid, remember?"

Her shoulder jostled his. That flicker of contact shot through him like a spark.

Not real, he reminded himself. *Not real.* Once he found a job, he would leave Herons Bay behind. Put his past, and all the parental disapproval that permeated it, behind him. Elizabeth was a part of that past.

She grinned at him, her hair tucked out of her face and hanging down her back, her cheeks still rosy pink. When she beamed like that, she shone brighter than a Christmas tree. As she always had.

Shadows suited Mark better. One more reason she wasn't for him.

Chapter Seven

Headphones in. Christmas music chiming. Muscle memory leading Elizabeth's feet on the short walk to the Kents' house. A new day in Herons Bay.

Earlier that morning, Melissa had texted: Time for a dress fitting today? xx Elizabeth had accepted quickly. Nothing else to do with her parents busy preparing breakfast for their guests. And she needed a distraction—anything to keep her from compulsively checking her inbox for casting news.

No outing with Mark planned until this evening, either. After the hours they'd spent together yesterday, he could undoubtedly use a break from her until then. By the time he'd left her parents' house last night, he'd turned quiet again. Distant. As if they hadn't connected at all.

She thought they had. Over breakfast, at the beach, in her parents' kitchen…she had opened up to him, more than she had to anyone in a long time. And he'd seemed to do the same. But maybe she'd just been in the right place at the right time. Maybe she could have been anyone.

That was how she felt auditioning lately. Interchangeable with all the other bright-eyed twentysomething hopefuls. Awful. Elizabeth cranked up her music. *Merry.* She needed to walk into the Kents' house merry, not mopey.

And here she was. Her mom hadn't been kidding about the Kents' decorations. Elegant garlands, red velvet ribbons and delicate white lights abounded, which must look stunning come nightfall. Elizabeth paused in front of their lawn, taking in her once second home. All the time she'd spent here from kindergarten to college came rushing back. Sleepovers and study sessions and parties; homecoming and prom photos, Andrew and Mark on hers and Melissa's arms.

Two-person plays, back when they were really little— Melissa writing a short script, which Elizabeth would eagerly perform with her. As they grew older, Melissa and Elizabeth would try their hand at writing real full-length plays—Melissa preferring to focus on dialogue, Elizabeth on the stage directions and blocking details. Not that those shows had ever seen the light of day. The directors of the Cranberry Players, Cecelia and Jill, had encouraged their efforts, but they didn't have the funding to put on plays written by two teenagers. She and Melissa had persevered, though. Just for the joy of it.

Her heart panged, but she summoned a smile. A straight spine. Nothing to do now but move forward— literally. She walked along the Kents' driveway to the front door and rang the bell. She'd always rung the doorbell as a kid, too, even though Mr. and Mrs. Kent had made it clear she was welcome anytime.

A moment later, the door swung open.

"Elizabeth Brennan," Mr. Kent said with a toothy grin. "Welcome back."

"Hi, Mr. Kent," she said, stamping down a sudden

onset of shyness with an extra notch of cheer. "Merry Christmas week!"

"Oh, you're not a kid anymore. Call me Ed," he said, encouraging her to take a step inside with a gesture of his arm. "I can't believe how grown up the two of you are. You off in New York. Melissa about to get married. You'll realize when you get to my age—time flies."

"Oh, I already feel that way," Elizabeth said with a small laugh.

He'd certainly made her life in New York sound like an accomplishment. No one in Herons Bay could have guessed that Elizabeth was feeling demoralized by city striving lately—not with the way she kept smiling through it.

Fake it until you make it. That was what Cecelia and Jill had advised her, years ago, when she'd told them of her Broadway hopes. Advice she'd followed to this day.

Glancing around the front hall, Elizabeth asked, "Where's Melissa?"

"Just getting off the phone about some new wedding travail. I tell you, I wouldn't blame the two of them if they up and eloped."

"Bite your tongue, Ed Kent." Mrs. Kent's voice broke in. The woman herself followed, turning the corner from the living room. "You'll scare the poor girl off before she's fully in the door."

A moment later, Mrs. Kent's gentle arms were enfolding her. "Good to see you, dear. It's been much too long."

"You too, Mrs. Kent." Elizabeth leaned into her shoulder before pulling away. "Your home is still as lovely as ever. As are the two of you."

"You're good for our egos," Mr. Kent said with a chuckle. "We've missed you around here."

"And call me Cheryl," Mrs. Kent said. "Please. I'm so thankful you're here. I couldn't understand why Melissa didn't ask you to be in the wedding from the start."

Elizabeth had some guesses. That they hadn't been good friends in years now. That it might be awkward for Elizabeth, given her history with the groom. That it might be awkward for Melissa, given Elizabeth's history with the groom. That it might be awkward for Andrew, given his history with Elizabeth. Mix, match and take your pick.

But Elizabeth didn't voice any of that. Instead, she said, "How could I say no when I heard you had a spare dress?"

"Talk about a sign from God," Cheryl agreed. "Melissa needed a good sign. All these wedding-day hiccups have started to weigh on her."

"Hiccups?"

"I'm sure Melissa will want to vent to you herself when she comes down. Do you want to try on that dress while we wait?"

Elizabeth nodded, thankful for something to do. "You're incredible, taking the time for this, with the wedding just a few days away."

"Remind my daughters of that, will you? They think I meddle too much."

Ed coughed on a laugh.

"Well, maybe I do," she ceded. "But that's a mother's prerogative, isn't it?"

"Oh, definitely," Elizabeth said.

"Just wait until you get married. Your mother will be just the same."

No doubt her mom was looking forward to helping her with wedding plans—if that day ever came.

Merry, she reminded herself, *not mopey*.

Fortunately, Melissa chose that moment to call down the stairs, "Coming! Sorry!"

Elizabeth turned just in time to see her oldest friend walking down the stairs. Even a stranger could have caught the stress lining her brow and pinching her eyes. She watched Melissa try to smile through it.

"Thank you so much for coming over," Melissa said with threadbare enthusiasm. "I hope I didn't interrupt your morning?"

"Not at all! Anything I can do to help."

She sounded a bit peppier than she'd intended. This was the version of her that had never interested Mark— the sunny persona that won over everyone else.

Melissa stood there for a moment, her eyes darting around the room, clearly still recovering from her phone call.

"Elizabeth was just about to try on Phoebe's spare dress." Mrs. Kent broke in. "Shall we?"

"Oh, perfect," Melissa said. "I can't wait to see you in it."

"I can't wait to see it," Elizabeth replied. Right now, all she could see was how fragile Melissa suddenly seemed. Melissa had always been delicate, but ethereally. Emotionally. Sensitive and petite, not brittle, as if a harsh wind rather than a word could break her in half.

Clad in a winter coat, hat and bulky sweater yesterday, Melissa hadn't appeared as waifish as she did today. Now, Elizabeth could see that a new thinness haunted her cheeks and waist, which she hadn't seen in any of her Instagram photos over the last year. A—wholly unnecessary— wedding diet? A recent bout of the flu? Anxiety?

Elizabeth shouldn't make any assumptions. She didn't know Melissa well enough anymore.

Melissa's mom led them out of the front hall, through the family room and into her sewing room. It doubled as a library, books lining the walls, and tripled as a game room, with weathered cardboard boxes filling the cabinets. The main attraction of the room, however, was clearly Cheryl's sewing setup. The well-used machine, the table topped with measuring tools and different colored threads, the half mannequin in the corner. She and Melissa hadn't been allowed in here when they were little out of worry they'd step on a stray needle.

"Dare I ask about the phone call?" Cheryl said.

"Phoebe's flight was canceled. Again."

"She still has days to get home, hon. It will work out." To Elizabeth: "My younger daughter has been teaching English overseas."

"Which is wonderful," Melissa said. "Obviously. Except, her flights home keep getting delayed, then canceled, which is not so wonderful. This is the third time this week. Overbooked flight. Weather. Mechanical issues. You name it. You really don't think it's a bad sign?"

Clearly, that question had been meant for her mom, who quickly answered, "Don't be silly. You know how unpredictable and chaotic travel gets this time of year. Phoebe's flight status doesn't change how much you and Andrew love each other. How happy you make each other."

Melissa chewed on her lower lip, nodding. Then she turned to Elizabeth. "You know our wedding planner got the flu over the weekend? She's completely out of commission. And our harpist sprained her wrist last week slipping on some black ice. Is this wedding going to be a complete disaster?"

Why was she asking Elizabeth? But the uncertainty in her old friend's eyes had her heart twinging. "I think it's bad timing," Elizabeth offered honestly. "These things happen in December—flu season, icy weather, travel mishaps. All that really matters is you and Andrew."

"Exactly." Cheryl nodded. "Listen to her, if you won't to me. You'll be married come Christmas. That's all that will matter to you when you look back."

"But why does this all have to happen now? Right before my wedding day?"

"Think of everything that God has blessed you with. Philippians 4:8," Cheryl said, before paraphrasing: "Think on what's true, honest, just, pure, lovely." Elizabeth's favorite Bible verse. Advice she could heed as well. "You have a whole town that can't wait to see you get married. A man who loves you madly. Family and friends who will do anything for you."

"I know." Melissa took a deep shaky breath. "I know."

Mrs. Kent took her daughter's moment of composure to retrieve a dark green dress from the closet. "Here you are, Elizabeth. Will you try it on? Melissa needs some cheering up."

Elizabeth accepted the hanger and the emerald velvet gown swaying from it. Fluttering sleeves. The waist cinched by a large bow. "This is beautiful."

"Just wait until you see the wedding dress."

"I'm wearing hers," Melissa said, fondness smoothing the lines from her face. "With a few alterations."

"I'm sure it's stunning."

"I hope Andrew thinks so," Melissa said, fretting her lower lip once again.

"Of course Andrew will think so," her mom replied. "I wouldn't have worn anything but the best for my wedding day. Nor would I allow either of my daughters to walk down the aisle in anything but the absolute finest. Now, go on, Elizabeth. You'll never try it on if you wait for a lull in this conversation."

At a loss for what she could say to ease Melissa's worries, Elizabeth took the opportunity to walk to the first-floor bathroom—just where she remembered it— and change in private. Rich green velvet enveloped her. She contorted to pull up the dress's zipper, carefully retied its bow and swished a step. Its hem swept the floor. Maybe a little too long. But Melissa had been right— she and Phoebe were still the same size, give or take a few inches. Some slight adjustments, and she hopefully wouldn't embarrass Melissa (or herself) in the photos.

"Oh, it suits you!" Cheryl said when Elizabeth returned to the sewing room.

"I told you it was your color," Melissa said, looking calmer now. "At least *this* worked out."

"Come over here, and I'll get started on hemming it. Wouldn't want you tripping down the aisle."

"Would very much like to avoid that. Thank you," Elizabeth said. "What will I need for shoes?"

"Nude heels? Do you have a pair at you parents' house?"

"Done. I was planning on wearing nude heels to the wedding anyway."

"Thank you." Melissa clasped her hands together in gratitude. "I needed this. And thank you, Mom, for the alterations—for everything."

Elizabeth stared at herself in the mirror as Melissa's mom pinned the dress's hem. This—she smoothed a palm along its skirt—this did suit her. Jewel tones were her best colors, and this emerald green made her eyes pop. She *felt* beautiful. Why did Mark's face flash through her thoughts at that moment? Why was she wondering if the sight of her in this dress could crack his cool exterior?

Clearly, audition stress was messing with her mind.

Melissa's phone rang, jarring Mark's face from her thoughts. A glance at the screen had her old friend's brow drawn again.

"I have to take this, but I'll be right back. Thank you, you two! You're the best!"

Elizabeth nodded, stuck in place until Melissa's mom finished her work anyhow. Cheryl glanced up at her. "I hear Mark Hayes is escorting you to the wedding."

Elizabeth met her eyes in the mirror. "I'm sorry to spring that on you last minute. Melissa told me Andrew's mom had to rearrange the seating chart for the reception."

Cheryl laughed as she worked. "Gina enjoys tinkering with it. It drove her nuts, everything that wedding planner had commandeered before she got knocked out by the flu. And we had to change it again when you joined the wedding party, anyhow. Don't you worry. We're all happy to hear the two of you found each other."

"Oh. Um. I'm not sure…" She didn't want to mislead anyone, let alone Melissa's mom, who had only ever shown her kindness. "I'm not sure it's that serious. We only reconnected recently."

"Well, whether you're attending together as friends or more, you're both such beautiful souls. I never understood why you couldn't get along as kids." She chuckled.

"Immaturity." Elizabeth smiled. "I was also a little insufferable when it came to show tunes."

When was the last time she'd sung with her teenage

enthusiasm? When had musical theater last brought her joy rather than stress?

"You were delightful! Ed and I always adored your voice. I hope you know we'll be the first in line to see you when your big break comes."

Elizabeth swallowed. Tears? Gratitude? Dread? "Thank you. That means so much."

It meant belief. It meant encouragement. It meant pressure. It meant fear. It meant…a lot.

Much of the day passed just like that, a blur of wedding bell worries. Elizabeth had only planned to stick around the Kents' long enough for her fitting, but Melissa seemed too distressed to abandon.

After Elizabeth had changed back into her jeans and turtleneck, Melissa had grabbed her hand and said, "You'll stay awhile longer, won't you? We can catch up."

How could Elizabeth refuse?

Catching up turned into calling harpists all over the states of Massachusetts, Rhode Island and New Hampshire, seeking out anyone who might have last-minute availability. For Christmas Eve. So far, no luck among those they'd reached, but with all the voice mail messages they left, hopefully someone would call back.

They checked on Phoebe's new flight booking periodically, too, confirming again and again that it was still set to depart on schedule. So far, so good.

But Melissa kept fidgeting. Her energy remained frantic. And Elizabeth didn't know what else she could do to help.

"Tell me more about what's going right," she said finally, sitting cross-legged on Melissa's childhood bed. Déjà vu kept gripping her. Though Melissa had moved out a few years ago now, her parents had left her room mostly untouched. A time capsule. A 3D memory.

"Philippians 4:8?" Melissa said with a hesitant smile. "I haven't been following my mom's advice, have I?"

No, she hadn't been focused on what was true, honest, just, pure or lovely. But Elizabeth couldn't fault her for that. She'd seen far worse bridezillas.

"I'm thankful Pastor Mike is going to marry us," Melissa said, starting to tick gratitude off on her fingers. "That I'm getting married here in Herons Bay. I know I used to daydream about a fancy Cape Cod wedding, but it's so much more special here, where we grew up. Everyone has been so happy for us."

Her shoulders were relaxing from their hiked tension, a real smile easing onto her lips. Good. This was good. Elizabeth gave a nod, not wanting to break Melissa's rhythm by replying aloud.

Melissa spun a strawberry blond wave around her finger. "People were skeptical, you know. When we first started dating. They were so used to—well, they weren't used to us."

Another nod. Clearly, she hadn't wanted to utter *you and Andrew* or *Mark and me*. Maybe that would have felt like bad luck to her, too. Elizabeth was just as happy avoiding that conversation.

"Mark is really okay with being in the wedding?" she asked suddenly. "I know he's never liked the spotlight…"

Elizabeth didn't feel right disclosing anything he'd shared with her, so she said, "The spotlight will be on you and Andrew. Don't worry about that."

"And I know Andrew and I hurt him," she carried on in a smaller voice. A still softer voice.

"That was a long time ago," Elizabeth said gently.

She hoped it came out gently, that Melissa couldn't hear what went unspoken: *You hurt me, too.* Bringing it up now wouldn't accomplish anything. Would only confuse things.

Contrary to gossip and speculation, Elizabeth had never resented Melissa for *stealing* Andrew from her. Even if they hadn't already broken up, people weren't wallets or phones. You couldn't steal a person. Andrew had made his choice, and Melissa had made hers.

And she'd chosen Andrew over her. Over their friendship. And then they'd never spoken about it. That was what still stung.

"I know," Melissa said. "I know. But—it's just that he's always had this thing about Andrew. There really wasn't a worse person I could have fallen for after our breakup. And then he went all those years without a girlfriend. It's such a relief that you two…serious or not… I'm just happy he has someone this week."

Elizabeth pushed her hair behind her ears and found another truth. "He'd hate us talking about him like this."

"You're right. You're right." A deep breath and then she carried on. "I worry Andrew and I started out doomed sometimes, that the way we handled things back then is catching up with us now."

"You know God doesn't work like that."

"But it would explain a lot about our wedding."

"Okay, timeout. Let's get back to gratitude," Elizabeth said. "We've strayed a little from the purpose of the exercise here."

Melissa ran a hand through her hair. "I'm being the worst. You must think I'm a complete ingrate, complaining about all this."

Not an ingrate. Just…stressed. Just scared. Dispro-

portionately stressed and scared, Elizabeth thought privately. "Have you talked to Andrew about how you're feeling?"

Within a second, Melissa's face shuttered. "I don't want him to see me like this. He's been preoccupied enough on his own lately." A pause. "Mark didn't say anything, did he? About Andrew?"

Elizabeth shook her head, glad to be able to honestly say, "No. Not at all." Not in regard to Melissa anyway.

"Well, that's something, I guess." Melissa shook her head. "Don't listen to me. Andrew and I are both wedding-jitter weird right now. We're fine, though."

Opening her mouth, Elizabeth searched for the right words. What were the right words here?

"Then you have nothing to worry about," she finally said.

Melissa smiled. But it didn't reach her eyes.

Chapter Eight

Mark arrived at Sweet Somethings before Elizabeth for their Tuesday evening "date." *Good.* All the better to fortify himself. He stood outside the shop hoping the crisp air would help him focus his thoughts.

She'd caught him off guard yesterday. She'd been catching him off guard since asking him for coffee on Sunday, if he were being honest with himself. There weren't many people that Mark felt comfortable baring his soul to, and he certainly hadn't expected Elizabeth Brennan to number among them. He couldn't allow her to number among them. Sure, she was kind. And understanding. And her woodland-green eyes widened when he spoke to her as if she were absorbing his words into her very soul. And, yes, drawing a true smile from her made his heart race.

He blinked, forcing himself back into the moment. He thought about the glinting sugarplum-pink lights in the candy shop window. The chatter of happy kids carrying sweets and homemade hot chocolate as they pushed out the store's door. Not about the woman he couldn't have a real future with. Even if Elizabeth had feelings for him, she'd only become one more person for him to disappoint in the long run, just like his parents.

"Hi there," Elizabeth's light voice chirped from behind him. "Fancy seeing you here."

Mark turned around to find her tapping on his shoulder, clad in that same pink marshmallow of a coat from yesterday with a light green turtleneck visible underneath. Like a peppermint candy cane. Her blond hair hung over her shoulders in twin braids, and she'd donned a Christmas-red lipstick, which only made her smile that much more eye-catching. That much harder for him to drop his gaze from.

No wonder Elizabeth wanted to become an actress—she was the kind of girl you only expected to see on a stage or a screen. And not just because of her looks. It was her energy. Something intangible, immutable.

"I'm sorry I'm a few minutes late," she added. "My parents needed an extra hand restocking the rooms with new towels."

"I haven't been here long." No reason to tell her he'd arrived early just to—what? Prepare himself for her as though she were an exam?

"Oh, phew. Shall we, then?"

Mark nodded, opening the door for her. Quite the group had assembled within, and not just to shop the handmade sour gummy seashells, cranberry clusters and dark chocolate peppermint cups. Behind the candy counter, this year's seasonal help was honoring one of Sweet Somethings' most beloved traditions—their candy-cane-making demonstration.

"It's a little hypnotic," Elizabeth whispered as they approached the counter, careful to stand behind any kids. Clearly, she didn't want to block anyone's view.

Mark nodded, though she probably didn't see. He couldn't look away, either. Behind the counter, a girl in a Sweet Somethings baseball cap spun candy around the large hook bolted to the wall. Again and again. He wondered how heavy it was, all that smooth cream-colored candy.

He'd seen this demonstration enough times to know what would follow. Eventually, the candy would be brought down from the hook and molded into a large loaf on the counter. Ribbons of bright red would be pressed along its sides. From there, they'd start pulling slender candy canes from that mass.

"I wouldn't have thought you'd be a fan of this," Elizabeth said quietly. "Mr. Pancakes Are Too Sweet For Me."

Mark felt the corners of his mouth turn into an almost smile. "Do you still spend the entire month of December sneaking candy canes, Brennan?"

Another fact about her, long forgotten, that came back to him now clear as day. Growing up, Melissa had spent the month of December mainlining hot chocolate. Elizabeth, meanwhile, had somehow always had a candy cane on her.

"I'm twenty-eight," she said very seriously. "I don't have to sneak them anymore."

A laugh stowed away under his next breath.

"Careful, Mark," Elizabeth teased. "Keep laughing like that, and people are going to start thinking you like me."

"Isn't that the point?"

"Right," she said.

Her smile dipped. He hadn't intended that. But he could hardly tell her the truth—that in just a day he'd started to fear liking her too much. That he needed the reminder of their arrangement more than she did. Elizabeth wasn't spending time with him for the fun of it. She was off-limits, and he couldn't handle another rejection just now, regardless.

From her pocket, he heard a wind chime phone alarm trill. She tensed, her hand immediately diving into her coat. Her impatience to check her phone reminded him of his own jittering nerves when waiting to hear back from the universities he'd applied to. Every time, his phone beeped lately, he hoped it would be with news.

Elizabeth tried to swipe at her phone with one of her mitten-clad fingers only to decide it was taking too long. Mitten off. Finger swiping quickly across the screen. The next thing he knew, she'd grabbed his hand, clasping it tight. Her fingers through his. The pulse of her wrist against his.

He felt suddenly very alive.

"Wish me luck," she said.

Mark didn't need to know what for to say, "Good luck."

Her hand tightened around his. Mark curled his fingers through hers, squeezing the sentiment for good measure. *Good luck.*

A second later, her grasp had loosened. Her eyes scanned the screen again, her cranberry lips parting.

"Oh," she whispered.

Mark waited for her to say something more. Instead, she went mute, still staring at her phone screen. Though he didn't mean to pry, she was standing right next to him, her phone held right in front of him. He could see that she'd opened an email, but he didn't read it. He wanted to read it.

"Good or bad news?" he asked finally.

Elizabeth shook herself from her trance, her braids swaying with the motion. "Can we…"

She didn't need to finish. Mark nodded, curled his fingers through hers again and guided her out of the store through the clusters of shoppers.

Once they'd left the buzzing shop and its sweet aroma of sugar and fudge and chocolate, he heard Elizabeth take a deep breath. Then a few more deep breaths. She didn't protest when Mark led her over to a nearby bench, just lowered herself onto it as if on autopilot.

His freed hand felt empty. Chilled. But that was just the weather.

"What happened?" he asked, sitting down beside her, seeking her gaze.

Elizabeth gave it to him gradually, picking her stare up from her boots. "I auditioned for a play last week, and I've been waiting for news since getting home."

His stomach sank. Though he was only just getting to know Elizabeth, he could say with some certainty this wasn't how she'd celebrate good news.

"They enjoyed my audition, but they don't feel I'm the right choice for the show," she coolly recited. "They'll keep me in mind for future productions. They thanked me for my time." A shrug of her shoulders. "I don't know why I'm surprised. I've gotten a million of these rejections now."

That was still hard for him to believe. This was Elizabeth Brennan, who had always achieved things so easily. Who had always seemed to attract success and smiles like a magnet. She wasn't supposed to struggle. She wasn't supposed to hurt.

"Doesn't make it any easier," Mark said, thinking

of his own rejections in his academic job search. "I'm sorry, Brennan."

Elizabeth nodded slowly, knotting her hands in her lap. "Thank you."

Without planning to, without giving himself permission, Mark wrapped an arm around her shoulders, pulling her into his side. This close, he could feel her shaking with unshed tears. He hated this. Couldn't this casting director have gotten in touch with her after the holidays? Why mar her Christmas like this? No way they'd be starting rehearsals in the next four days.

"I know I can't take it personally," Elizabeth said so quietly she was almost speaking under her breath, "but every audition makes it harder to remember that. I've been praying, looking to God, but it isn't getting any easier."

Mark's nod landed in her hair; her head fell to his shoulder.

When was the last time he'd held someone like this? Given comfort like this? When was the last time someone had sought him for comfort?

She didn't seek you, a hard voice grunted through his head. *You were just here. Convenient.*

Mark steeled his jaw and rubbed his gloved palm along Elizabeth's arm. He doubted she could feel it through her coat. But he had to do something other than sit here mute and helpless.

"Do you want me to take you back to your parents'?" he tried. Surely she'd prefer their company right now.

But Elizabeth picked her head back up and turned panicked eyes on him. "No. No. I don't want them to see me right now. They've always believed I can do anything, and…" she trailed off. Restarted. "The whole reason I left home was to act, but I haven't done anything in New York I couldn't do here. Like that woman Jenna said."

"Ignore her." He wasn't a motivational speaker. He wasn't a pep talker. But he could say with conviction, "She doesn't know you."

Elizabeth didn't reply. Nor did she shake off his arm. Nor did she move away. So Mark didn't, either.

"I don't want to go back to the B&B right now," she said eventually. Still too softly.

Okay. Mark nodded. Not okay. He was supposed to be maintaining distance from her. He wasn't supposed to say, "Let's get dinner, then."

She inhaled. She exhaled. She turned to him with a shaky smile. "Thank you, Mark."

His heart beat faster, its frantic rhythm warning danger. Mark held her through it.

Main Street didn't offer many dinner options. Daisy's Diner closed for the day after lunch. The local pizza spot was always packed with families, especially on prime winter break evenings like this one. Coastal Café served a few premade sandwiches, but Elizabeth needed something heartier. Something soul renewing. Some magic meal that would convince her she wasn't failing everyone she loved.

Mark had given her his keys and asked her to warm the car up while he ran a last-minute errand in town. And then he'd offered to drive her wherever she wanted for dinner. She must be pretty pathetic to have Mark Hayes catering to her like this. Elizabeth felt pretty pathetic. What a night to choose a red lip. She probably looked more like a sad clown than a leading lady.

She had nearly cried on Mark's shoulder. On Main

Street. It was one thing to cry on the subway—even if someone noticed, they wouldn't comment. They wouldn't know her. But here?

She should have waited until later to read the email in the safe solitude of her bedroom. She should still be enjoying the candy cane pulling demonstration right now, nibbling on a handmade treat. She should haven't let Mark see her like this. No one in Herons Bay was supposed to see this side of her. Even in New York, she only ever let herself fall apart in front of her roommate Tara. And that was because they'd met freshman year of college. Tara had already seen her at her messiest, her most heartbroken, and liked her anyway.

Was she heartbroken over this part, though? Or was it her pride that ached? Elizabeth couldn't tell—and that scared her more than any rejection. If she stopped striving for this dream that had sustained her for so long, what else did she have? What could she do that meant as much to her?

Pressing the Unlock button on Mark's keys, she followed the ensuing beep to the car Mark had described. Dark green. A little banged up from city living. Filled, she realized upon opening the passenger's seat, with books on its back seat. Classics like *Moby Dick* and *The Old Man and the Sea*, as well as titles she didn't recognize.

Elizabeth grabbed *Moby Dick*—another classic that had never made it off her to-read list—and flipped to the first page after turning the car on. A gust of heat hugged her.

Mark opened the driver's door a few minutes later and raised an eyebrow at her choice. "Cheery reading."

Elizabeth lifted a shoulder. "I don't know. It's a little

calming so far. Maybe I should take to sea—people still do that right?"

"Whaling is very illegal in North America."

"I know *that*. I don't want to kill whales. But there are other seafaring jobs."

"Note to self—keep Brennan away from commercial ports. I don't want to explain to your parents how you ended up on a scalloping expedition."

"You tease, but I could have missed my calling…" She wasn't teasing anymore. Not really. And she wasn't talking about sea voyages, either.

Mark paused, staring ahead at the residential streets and all their Christmas cheer. What she would give to feel so bright, so festive again.

"You didn't," he said finally. So much certainty. Elizabeth longed, more than anything, for that faith to resonate within her again. A second later, he added, "This is a onetime offer. Do you want to play some show tunes?"

She bit back a small smile. "I must seem really sad."

"Onetime offer," he repeated. "You'd be showing high school Mark."

A hiccup of laughter. "Well, when you put it like that…"

Plugging her phone into the car's auxiliary input, she scrolled through one of her favorite playlists.

"I reserve veto power," Mark said.

"I'd expect nothing less."

When she finally pressed Play, he shook his head in mock disappointment at the song's opening bars. "Missed your shot."

"I couldn't be that cruel to you. Not after how kind you've been."

She'd chosen a Christmas album instead. Something

joyful. Something, hopefully, that would get her back in the spirit of the season. Sure, her soul felt slightly crumpled, but if the Virgin Mary could survive all the tribulations she'd faced around Christmas, Elizabeth could stomach one more rejection.

Said stomach twisted painfully with a hunger that dinner might not satisfy. A longing.

Couldn't she?

Glancing out the window, Elizabeth realized they were leaving town, passing the Welcome to Herons Bay sign and driving over the bridge. The ocean unraveled on either side of them, moonlit and still, reflecting the Christmas lights strung along the guardrails.

"Where are we going?" she asked, belatedly. When Mark had started driving, she hadn't even wondered at their destination. Herons Bay had a catchall seafood restaurant—called the Daily Catch, in fact—just outside town.

"Do you trust me?" Mark asked.

"That is definitely something a serial killer asks before he takes someone to a secondary location. But yes."

Mark's lips slanted into that half smile of his again. "Thanks for the vote of confidence."

The thing was, Elizabeth didn't know that she had trusted him just two days ago. He'd been a rival from her childhood and then a blank from age eighteen onward. A convenient date stuck in the same spot as her, but not a friend.

Who could have predicted how much his presence would calm her? There wasn't another person in town Elizabeth could stand seeing her like this. With the way they'd competed back in high school, Mark Hayes was the last person she should face defeat in front of. What

made him different now? She shouldn't feel this comfortable exposing her insecurities to him. She should
have her standard sunny smile—*fake it until you make
it*—fixed securely onto her face.

Maybe it was because he'd never cared for her stage
smiles. Seemed to understand how she felt. Didn't seem
to judge. Elizabeth thanked God for guiding her to him.
Was this the reason her prayers had led her to ask Mark
to Melissa and Andrew's wedding? This moment, here
and now?

That email had opened a lot of boxes she would rather
have left closed through Christmas. How much more of
this she could handle. Whether she should keep auditioning. Whether she should stay in New York. What
she should *do* if not following the dream that had determined her every step since adolescence.

But for now, Elizabeth rested her temple against the
car window and watched the familiar scenes of the South
Coast pass by. These were the roads where she'd learned
to drive as a teenager. Where, once upon a time, she
and Melissa and Andrew and Mark had driven around
together.

She did remember the girl she'd been back then, eagerly belting show tunes from the passenger seat while
Andrew grinned, Melissa hummed along and Mark
groaned. So confident. So much faith. How disappointed
she'd be to see herself now. Back then, she'd known with
complete certainty exactly what she was meant to do.
She'd felt purpose every time she sang a show tune. Joy.
Now, doubt stole a solo in her every song. Fear.

"What's your favorite Christmas song?" Elizabeth
asked abruptly when Mark stopped for a red light. Des-
perate for a change of subject, if in her own head.

Mark's eyes lifted in contemplation, as if he might find an answer on his car's ceiling.

"You must have a favorite Christmas song."

"I like a lot of songs," he said.

"Fine, what's *a* favorite Christmas song of yours?"

"Anything from that Nat King Cole Christmas album," he answered finally. "Or Bing Crosby's."

"You're secretly sixty, huh?"

"I enjoy the classics."

Elizabeth laughed before admitting, "Me too."

Sure, she liked the Christmas covers of Mariah Carey and Phoebe Bridgers and Kelly Clarkson, but she had a soft spot for the albums her parents played during the holidays.

"I like the timelessness," Mark elaborated. "Knowing they've lasted for decades and will probably last more."

Elizabeth felt anything but timeless. An expiration date seemed to itch on her forehead, warning of the day she'd no longer be considered an ingenue. Was it approaching? Was it here?

Refocus. Don't dwell. Think positive.

Queuing up some Nat King Cole for Mark, Elizabeth tried to guess where they might be heading based on their route so far. That would keep her in the present, where God wanted her, rather than diving into dread.

"Are you taking me for tacos?" she asked. While Herons Bay didn't have a Mexican restaurant of its own, a neighboring town of theirs had a decent one.

"Nope."

"Hmm…seafood?"

Another almost smile. "That's cheating. We're in New England. Everywhere serves seafood."

"Come on," she teased. "I need a win."

Regret stole through her when she saw his not-so-concealed wince.

"Kidding," she added. Kind of.

"Five minutes, Brennan. You'll know in five minutes."

Squinting, Elizabeth tried to remember what dining options they'd find five minutes away. Somehow, she doubted he was taking her out for a scoop of vanilla at the creamery they were about to pass.

"Ooh," she said. "Portuguese!"

"Gold star," Mark said with a shake of his head. A quick grin. "Still the top student."

"I know my local restaurants." Sousa's Restaurant was a small, cozy, blink-and-you-miss-it establishment with a devout following. One of her old favorites.

They pulled into a free street parking spot right in front that a departing Subaru had just freed up. Hard as it was to stay positive, Elizabeth thanked God for that bit of synchronicity.

"I can't find Portuguese in New York that lives up to the food here," she said. "Which is unbelievable. New York has every kind of food."

"But the South Coast has a larger Portuguese population," Mark countered.

"Still makes me sad I can't order chicken Mozambique on Postmates." Pointedly, her stomach growled.

Mark, kindly, ignored the sound. "Shall we?"

Elizabeth's favorite thing about chicken Mozambique? It came with both rice and french fries.

"This is so good," she gushed after her next bite. Sousa's really nailed their Mozambique sauce—the spice and garlic and butter of it all sang in her mouth. Exactly what she needed.

Mark grinned at her over his steak. Shame that he didn't show his teeth more often. Who knew they were so white, so straight? Brooding and reserved worked for him, but *happy…*

Since reading the rejection email, Elizabeth's stomach had been churning. Now, it was fluttering as well. Not with fear. Not with dejection. But with *Don't think it, don't you dare.* If Elizabeth admitted butterflies, even to herself, she'd have to overthink them. And her heart was too bruised right now for her to spiral over all the reasons she wasn't allowed to fall for Mark Hayes.

No time for dating. Too much weird history. Not to mention he probably wasn't moving back to New York. Not to mention how much it would hurt if she let him in, let him see her, and he left.

Elizabeth took a large sauce-soaked bite of chicken, shutting off her thoughts.

"It's not a visit home unless I come here," Mark said.

Mouth full, Elizabeth gave an enthusiastic nod. Back to the present. Back to the moment. This was where God wanted people to stay—engaged in each second of their lives, not ensnared by worry.

"I tried to make this for Juliet and Ophelia during my nannying days," Elizabeth said between bites. She'd told him about them the other night after the hot cocoa social, after he'd mentioned again that she was good with kids. The compliment warmed her still.

"And?"

"It didn't quite live up."

"Are you telling me you couldn't make a Portuguese dish as well as be a Portuguese chef?"

"You tease, but I really tried!"

A silent laugh. An eyeroll—which would usually irritate her, except that she could swear affection lay behind it.

"Tell me about your favorite restaurant in New York," Elizabeth said, apropos of needing to think about something other than Mark Hayes's stormy sea eyes. "Please."

Mark chewed that over—literally. Once he swallowed, he said, "I don't know if I have a favorite restaurant. I like street food, though."

"Not Carbone?" Elizabeth teased, throwing out the most exclusive, pricey restaurant she could think of. They didn't take walk-ins, and a reservation required refreshing Resy at exactly 10:00 a.m. thirty days in advance.

"I want a long line, a street cart and halal or dosas to go. Not Carbone."

"I've never been," Elizabeth admitted. "Not quite in my price range. I like street carts, too, though."

"What's Elizabeth Brennan's favorite restaurant in New York?"

"I like the Greek food in Astoria a lot," she said. "I moved there last year, and there are so many amazing restaurants I'd never tried before. Back when I was nannying on the Upper West Side, I liked eating at the pier café at Riverside Park with Ophelia and Juliet—mostly for the view of the Hudson."

"It's something," he agreed.

"You've been?"

"Sure. We can't all nanny in Upper West Side town houses, but I was on the west side, too. I ran through Riverside Park all the time."

How strange, thinking that she could have run into Mark there any summer day as she enjoyed a burger by the river or studied a script on a park bench. Would they have reconnected? Or would he have been an awkward hello, an odd story, if she'd run into him in Manhattan?

"Still a cross-country runner then?" was her only reply.

"Won't be breaking my high school record anytime soon, but I jog."

Elizabeth was sure *jog* was an understatement. No doubt he could run circles around her. One only had to look at his well-muscled arms to know he kept in shape.

"I can tell," she said, without thinking. Her nerves were so frazzled, between her morning with Melissa and her evening of disappointment, her censor must have gone on the fritz.

Both of Mark's eyebrows shot up.

Elizabeth blushed. Furiously. And not because of the hot sauce in her Mozambique. "I mean, you were always so disciplined. Especially about running."

"Ah."

She ate several french fries, all the better to fight off her pink cheeks. All the better to avoid digging herself any deeper. With her next breath, she asked, "What's your favorite thing about New York during Christmastime?"

"Why do I feel like you're asking me icebreakers?"

"I might have prepped a few in advance. Before we met for coffee on Sunday." At the time, New York had been the only thing she'd known they had in common.

"Of course you did." Mark shook his head. "You answer this one first, I need to think."

Tilting her head, Elizabeth let her eyelids flutter shut and imagined the city in December.

"I like the really touristy things," she admitted. "Walking along Fifth Avenue to see all the stores and the Rockefeller Christmas tree. The Rockettes. The Christmas

Market at Bryant Park, and the window displays at the Macy's in Herald Square."

"Brennan. You're hurting me."

"I know, I know. They're crowded and cliché, and I love them. They're instant holiday cheer."

New York hadn't always been kind to her, but she loved it all the same. In a different way than she loved Herons Bay, to be sure. It was like comparing the Big Apple to fresh cranberries. She wanted both. Preferably in pancake form. With chocolate chips.

"Your turn," she prompted.

"I guess I'm not much of a Christmas season guy."

Elizabeth stared. "Mark. You're hurting me."

"I like the day. The opportunity to celebrate the birth of Christ. The smell of a pine Christmas tree. *It's A Wonderful Life.* But so much of it feels commercial. I don't see what's so festive about buying overpriced gifts in Bryant Park or fighting through a crowd at a Macy's."

She'd never thought about it like that before. Elizabeth didn't love those attractions because of their wares or sales. It was the effort, the festivity, the beauty, the Christmas music they set caroling through her head that sparked her joy. And, okay, also the morkie ornament Tara had bought for her in Bryant Park as an early Christmas gift. It looked so cute on the little tree they'd decorated in their apartment.

"And I sound like Scrooge," Mark said wryly.

"No," Elizabeth replied quickly. "You're right. The simple things are the most important. I just love the spectacle of the season, too. Trust me to like the showy things."

But she appreciated other things as well. The lights strung throughout Herons Bay. The holiday stroll on

Main Street that kicked off the month of December. Christmas Day with her parents. The buoy Christmas tree outside the church—each year, local businesses and classrooms and artists contributed a hand-painted buoy, which the church assembled into a tree. After Christmas, they auctioned the buoys off to the town for charity. So quintessentially New England.

"Shows make people happy," Mark said seriously. "Don't give up on that."

He'd said it a little too seriously. Somehow, Elizabeth didn't think they were still talking about Manhattan tourist attractions.

She took a long sip of her water. She didn't think of herself as a quitter, but what if she'd strayed from God's plan for her without realizing it? What if all these rejections were His way of nudging her down a new path?

She searched her heart for answers. But her heart was extremely preoccupied with Mark's earnest face in the flickering candlelight.

"Thank you for this, Mark," Elizabeth said finally. "I needed it."

A nod. "Anytime, Brennan."

Except, not really. She didn't know if they'd even stay in touch come the end of this week.

As comfortable silence settled between them, the intimacy of their dinner struck Elizabeth anew. A cozy corner table, dim lighting, a small candle blazing between them.

"Do you ever think of moving back here?" she asked, once again apropos of—by all appearances—nothing. "For real?"

His eyes widened, then narrowed. "Hard-hitting ice-breaker."

"I do sometimes. I love New York, but I don't see myself there forever."

"It's an expensive city," Mark carefully agreed.

Sure was. And that should probably have preoccupied Elizabeth more, but she continued, "And there are so many other girls there with the exact same dream as me." What was she contributing? How was she making a difference?

"There's no one like you, Brennan."

Heat stole over her face again. She couldn't do anything more than blink and murmur, "Same to you."

Mark stared at her, his gray-blue eyes unreadable. Then he looked down at his plate and said, "Right now, my only goal is to find an open position at a university. Whatever I find, that's where I'm supposed to be. But who knows what God has planned for the future?"

"'Take therefore no thought for the morrow,'" Elizabeth quoted Matthew's gospel.

"For the morrow shall take thought for the things of itself," Mark finished.

But what did you do when tomorrow came? She was worrying again. Even as she recited a Bible verse that explicitly warned against worrying. *Elizabeth.*

"I have another question," she said, clearing her throat.

"Oh, boy."

"This one is easy, I promise. Do you still have room for dessert?"

Mark leaned across the table, his face suddenly close to hers, his low voice, all at once, all she could hear. Never mind the noise from the kitchen and the vague conversations buzzing around them.

"I might have gotten a few things from Sweet Somethings while you warmed up the car earlier," he said.

"Candy canes?"

"Three or four."

"Oh, you're good." Thoughtful. Kind. So much more than she'd seen as a kid. "Thank you."

He was close enough to touch now. Close enough that she could feel his breath on her skin. Close enough to kiss. But Elizabeth stayed put, and he sat back in his chair, and it was really for the best. Really, really.

Mark Hayes wasn't hers to kiss. For all the reasons she'd already reminded herself of—their complicated pasts, their uncertain futures. More than that, though, she didn't think she could stand another rejection tonight. Elizabeth was clinging to her confidence by a fraying Christmas ribbon, and if Mark flinched away… if he revealed that pity had motivated him to take her out tonight…

The waiter brought the check over. Elizabeth told herself she was relieved the evening was coming to an end.

Then, Mark said, "Do you have plans tomorrow night?"

A breath caught in her throat. Elizabeth forced it forward. "With you, I think. Blue Heron Books, right?"

"I thought we could push that a day. If you don't mind another surprise."

Careful, her heart thudded. *Danger*.

"What do you have in mind?"

"A surprise. Do you trust me?"

Elizabeth could only nod. *Yes*.

Chapter Nine

Elizabeth's parents supplied their guests with overnight oats and bakery-bought pastries for breakfast the following morning. Which meant: the three of them could finally enjoy a family breakfast at Daisy's Diner.

"This is such a treat," her mom said as they claimed a booth by the front window. "I still can't believe we have you home for the holidays after all this time, the one Christmas we're booked solid."

"You're very in demand," Elizabeth agreed with a grin, crossing her legs on the blue leather seat, shrugging off her coat behind her. "Melissa says the guests are all thrilled."

She hoped no one noticed the extra concealer she'd applied this morning to hide her anxious, sleepless night. Fortunately, Elizabeth had acquired some makeup skills during her community theater days. She knew how to draw and deter focus.

"We're thrilled that you two are talking more again," her mom said. "I always thought it was a shame, the way you grew apart."

Me too, Elizabeth let herself admit. Aloud, she said, "She just needs help with some last-minute wedding things—neither of you can think of a harpist who'd have holiday availability, can you?"

His dad furrowed his brow. "I can't think of a harpist full stop."

Her mom didn't look any more certain. "Not off the top of my head, either."

"The one she booked sprained her wrist last week. And her wedding planner is down with the flu, so…"

Elizabeth trailed off when she noticed Mark and his family reflected in the diner window in a booth across the room. A fun house mirror of her own family, with his parents on one side of the booth and Mark on the other. He took what appeared to be a bracing sip of coffee.

"Best of luck to her. Not the easiest time of year to find last-minute availability," her dad said as he looked at his menu—even though he'd been ordering the same exact dish here for as long as Elizabeth could remember. Crab cake eggs Benedict every time. "But I'm sure someone will come through."

Without planning to, Elizabeth felt herself rising to her feet, propelled by the traitorous fluttering in her stomach.

"I'll be right back," she murmured to her parents as they perused the menu. "Will you order the waffles for me? I want to say hi to Mark and his family real quick."

"Take your time," her dad said, with a wave of his hand. "I need another minute with the menu anyway. Never know. Might shake it up today."

"I'll believe it when I see it," her mom said to him. "Say hi for us, Lizzie. I can't remember the last time we caught up with Carolyn and Doug…"

Making her way across the diner, Elizabeth wove around waiters and guests and the eager patter of her own heart. Mark noticed her approaching first. He lifted his coffee mug in a tacit hello, but didn't look entirely jubilant to see her.

Elizabeth told herself he wasn't a morning person, and summoned her friendliest smile for his parents.

"Hi there," she said. "I just wanted to say good morning."

Mark raised a brow at her. She shrugged back. It was a small town. She was bound to bump into his parents eventually—definitely at the wedding if not sooner. Why not get ahead of it?

It struck her how much time had passed since she'd last conversed with Mr. and Mrs. Hayes. Occasionally, she bumped into them around town when visiting Herons Bay, but she'd never known them well enough to exchange more than a quick hello. Once she and their nephew had broken up, topics of small talk had dried up fast.

"Elizabeth Brennan," his mom said, setting her mug on the table. "It's been ages. How are you doing?"

"Thankful to be home for the holidays. How are you, Mrs. Hayes?"

She'd never realized just how closely Mark resembled his mom. The same piercing eyes. The same angles to her face. The same waves in her dark hair. From his dad, he'd inherited a long, straight noise and broad shoulders. In the past, she would have said they shared a certain coldness, too, but Elizabeth knew better now. Knew Mark better.

"Enjoying all this time with our son," Mark's mom said. "The best Christmas gift I could ask for—though I know he's chomping at the bit to get back to a college campus."

"I wouldn't say *chomping*," Mark inserted.

"Your parents must love this time with you, too," she carried on. "Are you home long?"

"Not long enough," Elizabeth said with a levity she didn't feel. "Just through the weekend."

"What a shame," his mom said, with what seemed to be a warning glance at Mark. "You know, Mark probably won't be moving back to New York."

"I—"

"Elizabeth knows, Mom."

"Oh, of course she does. You two would have talked about that already."

He gave her an apologetic look, but Elizabeth couldn't blame his mom for her concern. No mother wanted to see her son hurt by a messily ended romance. *So-called romance.*

"I'm excited for him. I'm sure he'll end up somewhere wonderful." Somewhere far away probably—a good reminder for her. Even if something had sparked between them, she'd never try long distance again. And auditioning left her fragile enough. Trying with Mark, failing with Mark, might undo her.

Distressing thoughts. Pointless thoughts. She and Mark had reconnected mere days ago. They knew what they were doing.

She looked to his dad rather than examine the twinge in her chest. "How are you doing, Mr. Hayes?"

"Just fine." A blank face. A sip of his coffee.

Elizabeth waited to see if he'd elaborate from there. Apparently not.

"I won't linger too long," she said. "But I wanted to thank you for letting me steal your son so often this week. His company has been a huge blessing."

"He has plenty of time to steal," his dad said. "No work or wedding to keep you busy this week, eh, son?"

She watched as Mark's fingers tightened around his mug. "Nope."

Okay then. Either his dad had a harsher sense of humor than Elizabeth understood, or she'd stepped on a minefield. She rallied with a laugh.

"None for me, either, obviously. And there's only so much I can do to help my parents at the B&B—they have their routine set. I'm really thankful to Mark for putting aside his research to spend time with me."

"He should be taking some time to relax," his mom said. If she noticed anything odd about her husband's words, she didn't let on. "I keep telling him, academics are supposed to get a winter break."

"He deserves it," Elizabeth said, earning a slight eyebrow raise from Mark. She could practically hear him saying, *Really?* "I can't imagine the work it takes to finish and defend a dissertation."

So what if she was being a little heavy-handed with her praise. His dad's dig had felt heavier-handed.

"Neither can we." His mother smiled. "Doug and I never thought we'd have a professor in the family."

His dad opened his mouth, and Elizabeth prayed for something positive to follow. "Used to think he might follow me into dentistry someday. But Mark's never been the practical sort."

It took resolve to keep her smile in place. Though she knew it was time to wrap things up—this clearly wasn't going well—she had to say something.

"You must be proud," she repeated. "A PhD at Mark's age takes a lot of passion and persistence. But it's no surprise. He was always one of the smartest students in our class."

His mom smiled. His dad gave a curt nod. Elizabeth took her cue to leave. She'd tortured Mark enough with this conversation, judging by the death grip he'd curled around his mug.

"I'll leave you to your breakfast. I just wanted to thank you for letting me monopolize Mark this week. He's been the best date."

"Pleasure catching up with you, Elizabeth," Mark's mom replied, voice as pinched as her smile. "We'll see you at the wedding."

Elizabeth said a brief goodbye to Mark before extracting herself, but his face remained expressionless. Impenetrable once more.

"What a nice girl," Mark's mom murmured as Elizabeth walked away, her blond ponytail swinging with her every step. More power to her for not running.

Meanwhile, Mark sat very still. Very stiff. His mind was a miasma. *Why didn't you say more? Why didn't you defuse the tension? Why didn't you help her? Why didn't you at least smile at her?*

Everything she'd said in his defense echoed through Mark's head. The drive and passion he'd waited years for his parents to recognize in him, she'd seen. Celebrated. Like they were obvious. What did it say about him that praise left him so speechless? Hers especially.

At the very least, he could have warned Elizabeth that pleasantries with his parents were pointless. Sure, his dad had liked her enough on Andrew's arm. But on his? Trust Doug Hayes to prove the contrarian.

Case in point: "But not the girl for Mark."

"Oh, Doug." His mom sighed. But she didn't argue, either. Clearly, Elizabeth's impassioned faith in him hadn't resonated with his parents.

His dad shook his head. "All the Herons Bay girls who Mark could have reconnected with, and he chooses his cousin's ex-girlfriend. Who lives in New York. I just don't get it."

Now he'd been relegated to the third person in this rerun of a conversation. *Great.* Mark could have reminded his dad—again—that Andrew and Elizabeth had dated nearly a decade ago now. Or that Andrew was hopefully too busy getting married to care whether Mark was interested in his high school girlfriend. Or that he'd also lived in New York up until a month ago and could possibly wind up moving back. But what was the point? Mark was tired of knocking on the brick wall of his dad's disapproval again and again, never making headway, only ever bruising the knuckles of his self-esteem.

This was why he hadn't told his parents about the unexpected communication he'd had with the English Department at a university in Chicago earlier this morning. Not while it still had a question mark tacked onto the end. He couldn't bear his mom's obvious doubt or his dad's disapproval any longer.

If Elizabeth couldn't un-lodge a single brick of it for him with her sunny smiles and charm, what chance did he have? She was like vanilla ice cream or birthday cake, universally palatable to the people of Herons Bay, unless you had a problem with sweets. Which, as it happened, his dad did.

"What your father means," his mom said, dousing her coffee with an uncharacteristic amount of sugar, "is that we want you to find the right person. We know how hard this season of your life has been. We'd hate to see you get more hurt."

Her words from the other night echoed again. *Sunshine burns.* She wanted him to find someone safer.

All Mark could do was repeat what he'd told her earlier. "You don't need to worry about that. It's not serious."

Nevertheless, worry lingered on his mom's features. Satisfaction set his dad's. And Mark, well, Mark forced himself to keep his eyes on his table rather than Elizabeth. Forced his expression blank of anything at all.

He could picture her sitting with her family enjoying pancakes, though he still didn't let himself look. His imagination could paint Elizabeth's goldspun hair, her laurel eyes, her true smile, no trouble.

Another image followed, unwise and unbidden. Sitting across from her at Sousa's Restaurant. Elizabeth's face so close to his at one point. The breathless gap between her pink lips. The blush on her cheeks. The ease with which he could have reached across the table and touched either of them… and risk shattering the moment. Ruining their unexpected connection.

If his own parents couldn't love him without conditions, why would anyone else? Why would Elizabeth? If he reached for more, if she gave it to him, she would become one more person capable of wounding him with her eventual disappointment or disinterest.

Better to leave Elizabeth where she was—in his periphery, in his memory, untouchable.

Elizabeth was in trouble.

When Melissa had texted her after breakfast to see if she might be able to try on her bridesmaid dress again, just to make sure it didn't need any other changes before

Friday, Elizabeth had said yes. Immediately. Of course. She welcomed any distraction from the fear squirming in her stomach.

Yesterday's rejection, after the countless ones she had received, shouldn't have affected her this way. Was it her parents' proximity? The questions around town of whether she'd *made it* yet? The hominess of Herons Bay penetrating her city-living armor? In New York, she grinned and bore the audition cycle, but had that become simple habit? Auditioning was such a part of her routine, a given in her city existence, that Elizabeth never let herself consider the alternatives. What had all this effort been for if not Broadway? A career on the stage? How else could she channel her passion?

Home for a few days, though, without a monologue to memorize or a dance to learn…without an open call to rush to…

Elizabeth couldn't remember the last time she'd allowed herself to question the dream she'd picked out at age four. Who was she if not an actress?

Uncomfortable question. Impossible question. She'd prayed that a dress fitting might drag her out of her own head, her mosquito-bite worries. Instead, she'd found herself plunged into Melissa's.

They'd headed to Coastal Café shortly after Elizabeth's arrival at the Kents'. The latest wedding upset had Melissa's parents insisting that their daughter get out of the house for some fresh air, a change of setting. So Melissa had decided they'd get coffee.

"Can you believe it?" The bride was spiraling, massaging her temples with two fingers. "Phoebe finally flies out of Madrid. And then her connecting flight gets canceled! I don't understand how this keeps happening."

"Where does that leave her now?" Elizabeth asked, sipping her gingerbread latte.

"London. Waiting on the next available flight to Boston or Providence."

Poor Phoebe. How much time had she spent stuck in hectic airports now? Where had she been sleeping? Had she checked a bag? Where had *that* ended up?

If Phoebe still resembled the kid from Elizabeth's memory, she'd be rolling with the punches. Making friends with her fellow travelers. Accumulating stories for the road. A bit younger than Melissa, Phoebe had been an underclassman in high school when they'd graduated. A free spirit, though, even then. Eclectic thrift shop clothing, sourced from trips into Boston. Elaborate braids and updos. Travel posters on her walls. No wonder she'd spent her first few years of postgrad life teaching English abroad. Her social media spoke of constant adventure.

"That's progress." Elizabeth tried to play the cheerleader. "One flight and she's here. She has two more days."

Melissa nodded even as her lower lip trembled. "Flights are just so booked. I know she's trying her hardest to get home and that she doesn't want to be stuck in an airport right now either and that she feels horrible, even though none of this is her fault, but…" A ragged breath. Watery eyes. "She's going to be jet-lagged at my wedding, Elle. If she even gets here in time!"

"Melissa. Breathe," Elizabeth said, leaning across the table to cup a palm around her old friend's shoulder. She tried to pack as much comfort into that touch as she could.

Melissa sighed. "I sound like a total bridezilla, don't I?"

"Anyone would be emotional right now. You get to cry if you need to."

"Probably not the place for it." A teary snort. "I promise, I'm really trying to follow my mom's advice and focus on the good. Not very well, but I *am* trying."

"I get it. It's easier said than done." Oh, did she get it.

"Never mind maid of honor—she's my *sister*. I can't get married without her."

"I don't think you will." *Please, Heavenly Father.* Elizabeth knew that God wasn't a genie, that prayers weren't wishes on a lamp, that sometimes struggle served a purpose, but she still prayed for Phoebe to make it home in time. For Melissa to have the wedding of her dreams.

A beeping noise vibrated from Melissa's purse, interrupting her thoughts.

"I'm sorry," she said, once she'd grabbed her phone from its depths. "It's my mom. I'll only be a second."

Elizabeth nodded.

When Melissa pressed her phone to her ear, Elizabeth could hear her mom's muffled voice through its speaker. "Now, honey, don't freak out—"

That did not bode well.

Mouthing *I'll be right back* to Elizabeth, Melissa stood to take the call outside with very stiff shoulders. A very drawn brow.

Though she didn't want to spy, Elizabeth couldn't help but watch her old friend out the coffee shop window. Her hair had gone staticky against her sweater, its ends levitating off her back. She was using her free hand to massage her temple again.

That really did not bode well.

Unsure of what Melissa was hearing, still less sure of how she could help, Elizabeth hurried over to the counter and quickly ordered a brownie—Melissa's favorite dessert from childhood. The number of times they'd hung out at one of these tables, a huge, powdered-sugar-sprinkled brownie between them after a bad day came rushing back to her now. Granted, this was a little higher stakes than a C+ in physics.

By the time Elizabeth returned to their table, Melissa had reclaimed her seat. She had her elbows on the table, her forehead in her hands.

"I come bearing a brownie?" she tried. A peppermint candy cane brownie in fact, a special from the café's seasonal menu.

"I don't have a wedding cake," Melissa said dully. She stared into space, speaking in a monotone as if the panic had been knocked out of her.

"It's late?"

"It's lost. They lost our order. No record of it. I've lost my wedding planner, my harpist, my sister and now my four-tier winter white buttercream cake with pine cone and cranberry adornments."

Elizabeth blinked. Processing. Okay. Okay. As long as the bakery could provide a substitution…

"And the bakery doesn't have the availability to finish it before Friday now. Or a ready-made cake that will feed all our guests," Melissa continued, still sounding as though she were reading from a script. She reached blindly for the brownie between them and broke off a nibble. "This is perfect. Thank you. You're the one thing that's gone right this week."

"I didn't do anything. Right place, right time, right size," Elizabeth said, shrugging off the compliment. Literally. She couldn't help it. Sharing a dress size with Phoebe hadn't taken any grand skill or sacrifice on her part.

"Don't do that." Melissa eyed her now. "We've barely seen each other in years. You didn't have to agree to be in the wedding or come to coffee with me today or listen to…any of this."

Elizabeth's tongue curled around a parade of denials— *Don't worry about it, I don't know what you're talking about*—but she forced herself to sit with those words instead.

"Melissa, you're getting married. We might not be as…well, as close as we used to be. But do you really think I'd want to be anywhere else?"

The truth behind the sentiment throbbed through her chest. Despite her discomfort and reluctance and occasional resentment at the timing, Melissa's wedding mattered. The years they'd spent as best friends, the hours they'd devoted to daydreaming about their futures, meant something to her.

So things hadn't turned out exactly as they'd thought. Elizabeth didn't have a career in theater. Melissa hadn't become a playwright. But Melissa's dream wedding was still within grasp, and she was going to do everything she could to help her reach it.

Darting a look around the café, as if scanning for possible eavesdroppers, Melissa lowered her voice. "Part of me still thinks I deserve this. For the way Andrew and I got together."

"Melissa, no," Elizabeth said. Beneath her sweater, her heart hammered. She'd always wondered about that. Feared it had been while she and Andrew were still dating. Not that she believed her friends would have ever betrayed her that way. But when had their feelings for each other started brewing? "You didn't do anything wrong."

"Not technically. But I know I hurt you. And Mark. I should have had a real conversation with you…"

"This is all in the past. Years in the past. Don't mention it." *Please don't*. Elizabeth didn't want to unbury this, didn't want to dig past the scars. What if they opened anew?

Melissa twisted an errant wave into an anxious curl around one finger. "I wasn't pining for Andrew in high school, you know. I was loyal to Mark. And you."

Okay. They were doing this. After all this time. "I know."

"It wasn't like… I wasn't waiting until we went to college to steal him from you. Everything was just so big and new, and he was there."

And she hadn't been.

"And he needed a friend, too. One minute, he's the star lacrosse player and artist at Herons Bay High, and the next, he's an unknown freshman among thousands. He seemed more vulnerable to me than he ever had before. More real."

That would have been when he'd started feeling more and more remote to Elizabeth. Less and less real with her. Upbeat phone calls that never cut to the core of the new distance between them. Passively jealous texts— asking about the new faces in her Instagram photos, only to feign nonchalance when Elizabeth assured him they were just friends. He'd never told her that he was struggling. From his calls and texts, anyone would think he was living the dream. Which had made it that much harder to share her loneliness, her homesickness.

By the time they'd broken up over Thanksgiving, it had felt inevitable. They hadn't held a real conversation in at least a month. They couldn't last four years like that.

"I'm glad you had each other. I just wish—" Elizabeth faltered, the instinct to arm herself with a smile and a reassurance strong. She resisted it. Melissa was being real with her; she could give her the same, no matter how her throat tried to close around the words. "I just wish that it hadn't felt like you were choosing him over me. I knew Andrew would move on when we broke up. Losing your friendship came out of left field."

She'd never articulated that before. Not to anyone except God.

Melissa's loose wave had morphed into a tight coil of hair around her finger. She released it, only to start twirling those frazzled strands again. An old tic. "I didn't mean to. Choose him over you, I mean."

Elizabeth nodded.

"I was guilty, though. And insecure. I was always the behind-the-scenes girl, and you were always the star, and I liked it that way. Until I started dating your ex. You became this reminder of everything else Andrew might want."

"I hope you're not still worried about that?" Elizabeth joked weakly. "You've got some pretty compelling evidence on your ring finger that you don't need to."

Melissa's laugh sounded forced. Elizabeth couldn't blame her. Nothing about this conversation was coming easily to her, either.

"I wish we could have talked about this back then. I never meant to make you feel like that," Elizabeth said. "As for the rest of it...you didn't do anything wrong, and your wedding is going to be beautiful. We should start calling around for alternate cakes, though."

Pulling her notebook from her bag, Elizabeth flipped to a clear page and started listing bakeries she remembered in the area. She'd search online next, add those findings to her list and then check them off one by one as they called.

"I missed you, Elle."

Elizabeth found her efforts at organization momentarily paused when Melissa grabbed eye contact with her.

"I'm really glad you're in my wedding. Maybe— maybe this can be a restart for us."

Words clogged her throat, too many, too thick to say. Elizabeth nodded. "Me too."

Connection. Hope. Renewal. All three bubbled through Elizabeth, lifting her spirits. By the time they started scrolling through their phone in earnest for alternate bakery options, Elizabeth had no trouble believing they'd find someone who could pull this off.

"Um, excuse me?"

They both turned at the sound of a hesitant voice. A woman, the same one they'd bought their beverages and brownie from today, the same one Elizabeth recognized from her ill-fated coffee date with Mark, stood beside their table, wringing her fingers. Dark hair scooped into a bun. Cheeks tinted peppermint pink. Roughly their age.

"Hi," Elizabeth said. Did Melissa know her? She'd been away from Herons Bay long enough now to miss some new arrivals, but Melissa smiled blankly as well.

"You don't know me," the woman added. "If you're wondering. My name is Kristen. I just moved here."

Melissa introduced herself and Elizabeth before adding, "I've seen you around church the last few weeks. Usually, I'd have said hi there, but things have been a little…much lately. Let me belatedly welcome you to Herons Bay. Are we being too loud?"

"No! Not at all. I wouldn't usually interrupt, only… I overheard that you're looking for a wedding cake? I promise I wasn't eavesdropping, I was just—well, standing right over there." A nod to the counter.

"Yep," Melissa said, closing her eyes as if in pain. "I'm getting married in two days, and I need to find a new wedding cake."

"Well," the woman began, "I'm a baker. And, if you don't mind trusting a total stranger with your wedding cake, I'm happy to help."

Elizabeth had not been expecting that. But why not? She had just been thinking that God would provide.

"Really... Are you sure?" Melissa asked. She did not sound sure. "You really want to toil away on a wedding cake this close to Christmas?"

"I love baking. I'm good at baking. I'm also new here. I could use the good press of a wedding. I can send you my Instagram if you want. I have some videos and photos up there."

It boded well that she spoke the words "good press" with utter certainty. A wedding could also make for markedly bad press, after all, if she didn't finish in time or if the completed cake didn't pass muster.

"Do you have any samples I could try?"

Kristen pointed to the nearly decimated brownie in the center of the table. "That, for one. But I can get more..."

"Sit down," Melissa said, a hesitant smile unfurling onto her lips. "Let me tell you what I was thinking."

Chapter Ten

By the time Elizabeth and Melissa departed Coastal Café later that afternoon, they'd secured a cake. Not the exact one Melissa had ordered originally. She and Kristen had agreed that, given the limited time frame, a smaller wedding cake would make the most sense, along with a sheet cake to serve behind the scenes to most of her guests. But she was getting her white cake, vanilla buttercream, pine cones and cranberries.

God bless mysterious new-to-town bakers who didn't mind spending the days leading up to Christmas in the kitchen. Elizabeth still couldn't believe that had happened. She couldn't imagine a stranger in New York ever making such an offer—she couldn't imagine trusting them if they did. But Herons Bay was special.

One problem sorted. Hopefully, Phoebe's flight would land in Boston tomorrow morning, and that would solve another. And they just had to trust that God had a musician in mind for the wedding, too.

Still, Melissa hadn't stopped that nervous hair twirling of hers. Hadn't relaxed. Oh, she'd thanked Kristen profusely, but her eyes hadn't reflected the relief in her words. Then again, she'd never done well with stress or last-minute changes. Elizabeth supposed she was handling all these wedding-week woes remarkably well, considering.

All said and done, Elizabeth had made it home with just enough time to feed and walk Mary Tyler Morkie, eat dinner with her parents, don a dress that seemed versatile enough for whatever mysterious outing Mark had planned for tonight and redo her hair. Her braids had crinkled it into frantic waves, but she had it smooth by the time she walked downstairs.

"The nerve of that Mark Hayes," her dad said with a grin and a playful shake of his head, "stealing my daughter away on Christmas Eve Eve… Eve."

"Our favorite holiday of the year," Elizabeth said wryly. She felt like a teenager again, waiting in her parents' living room for her date to pick her up. Not that this was a date.

"I, for one, am excited to hear where he's taking you," her mom said, MTM curled up happily in her lap. "Not a dinner date… I just can't guess."

"Not a date at all," Elizabeth corrected. The words pinched, like jeans that still zipped but didn't quite fit. "I already told you, we're going to this wedding as friends."

Allowing other wedding guests to believe what they would—fine. But Elizabeth couldn't mislead her parents.

Her mom ignored that. "Will you text me when you find out? Now, don't pull your phone out while you're with him. But wake me up when you get home if I've fallen asleep."

"I won't be out that late," Elizabeth promised. As her mom had mentioned, there weren't many places to go in

Herons Bay after dark other than dinner. "But, yes. I'll tell as soon as I get home."

Ice cream? Possible. But most of the local creameries had closed for the season. A drive to look at the Christmas lights? More probable. But they'd already done some of that last night on their way home from dinner...

A knock sounded at the door. Elizabeth felt it in her chest. Mary Tyler Morkie must have, too, because she leapt down from her mom's lap to dart toward the door. She paused briefly to throw an indignant glance back at Elizabeth. *Aren't you coming?*

"We'll be right back," Elizabeth said with an indulgent glance at her dog.

"Please, bring him in," her mom said. "We'd love the chance to say hello again."

Moving toward the door, it hit Elizabeth anew how surreal it was that she was going out tonight with Mark Hayes. Thinking back on their school days, she realized how much time had passed. Elizabeth felt very old. Very far removed from them. But maybe that was for the best. Her friendship with Melissa looked different now but was hopefully healing. And as for Mark...

They had judged each other so unfairly. As idyllic as those teenage years had been, she and Mark had spent them in competition and ambivalence. She was thankful for Mark's friendship now. For the reminder that *change* didn't always mean *bad*.

Elizabeth twisted the front door open. Mark stood on the other side of the threshold, just as she'd expected. Less expected: the warmth that rushed through her when she saw him, even as cool air crept inside. Dark curls brushed his forehead, poking out from a pom-pom-less hat. Underneath his open coat, she could see a dark red sweater that contrasted handsomely with his gray-blue eyes.

He'd changed, too, she realized. From breakfast. Why did that make her blush? Why did everything make her blush lately? At this rate, she wouldn't need to replace the dwindling peach powder she'd been meaning to buy again at Sephora.

"Come inside," she said, holding the door open for him. "If we have time. Also, hi."

Mary Tyler Morkie said hi as well with her wagging tail, a soft whine and a twirl at Mark's feet.

"Hi," he echoed, with a half smile, revealing a bakery box he'd been holding under his arm. "We have time. I brought these for your parents, actually."

Elizabeth gasped at the familiar pink box. The logo printed on its side. A coffee cup swaying on an ocean wave. "You went to Coastal Café." By how long had they missed each other?

"I did," he said solemnly.

"And you didn't get me anything?"

"There are four cookies in here."

"Bless you."

Mary Tyler Morkie lost it at the word *cookie*, doing still more twirls, wagging her tail faster still. Mark handed his box off to Elizabeth and bent down to pet her finally.

"Hello, Mary Tyler Morkie," he said. "Yes, it's good to see you again, too."

Elizabeth grabbed a dog treat from the jar on the front hall counter and handed it to down to MTM.

At Mark's askance look, she explained, "We have this system where, when someone says the word *cookie*, she gets one."

Mark's brow lifted.

"I didn't create this system. She did."

"Your dog trained you."

"Yes. But I also blame my roommates—they're always baking—" she looked down to her happily munching dog "—*c-o-o-k-i-e-s*. Including ones for dogs, made from seaweed. I think they spoiled her while I was out."

"She hasn't mastered spelling?"

"Not yet."

"Brennan. Your dog is insane."

Finishing her treat, Mary Tyler Morkie gave a grunt of thanks and then ran back into the living room. No doubt to jump back up onto her mom's lap.

"Yes," Elizabeth agreed fondly.

Shaking his head wryly, Mark pulled off his hat. "How wild is my hair?"

It's perfect. But that was a silly thing to say to someone you weren't dating, so Elizabeth went with "You look great."

His cheeks were pink. As much as Elizabeth would love to believe she had done that to him, that they'd both caught the blushing bug, the cold seemed the more likely culprit.

"Is that Mark Hayes I hear?" her dad called from the other room. As if another Mark might have come to see her tonight.

She mouthed *Thank you* to her not-a-date before leading him into the living room.

"Evening, Mr. and Mrs. Brennan," Mark said. "Thank you for letting me take your daughter out this evening. And for the hot chocolate the other night."

Did Mark realize he sounded like he was taking her

on a date in a black-and-white film? Heat forced its way to her face again.

"It is and was our pleasure," her mom said.

"What my wife said. Feel free to call us Jane and George, though. We're all adults here." A grin. "Unless I should be calling you Dr. Hayes?"

"I'll leave that to my students," Mark said. "When I have students."

"Don't rush yourself." Her dad waved a hand. "You've achieved quite a milestone. A little time to relax never hurt anyone. I'm sure a bookworm like you has quite the reading list to conquer, after all those years of school."

"Just a few," Mark said with a half smile. "Thank you."

"And I'm sure your parents are thrilled to have you home," her mom added.

And the smile dropped, his mouth a straight line once more. He set the bakery box upon the coffee table. "I brought these for the two of you. Hoping you share your daughters' sweet tooth."

"We gave it to her," her mom said. "Poor thing. Thank you, Mark, you didn't need to bring us anything."

Her dad opened the box, examining the assortment of cookies. From the looks of it, a dark chocolate peppermint, a classic chocolate chip, an oatmeal raisin and a red velvet. Kristen's work?

"Don't listen. All guests have a mandatory—" a cautious glance at the dog on her mom's lap "—*dessert* tax now. Effective immediately."

Laughter shook her mom's shoulders. Elizabeth forced her eyes from that red velvet cookie. "Save one for me, please. At least half of one?"

Her dad was already biting into the chocolate chip.

Her mom smiled at her. "We'll see, Lizzie."

A little more small talk, and then Elizabeth was making their excuses, reminding her parents that they had to get on their way, though she didn't know where. In the front hall, Mark put his hat back on. Elizabeth threw on a coat and rushed to his car, eager for its heat.

He got in after her. "I had no idea you hated the cold so much." Amusement played at his mouth as she pulled her scarf up to her chin. "You know you live in New York, right?"

"It's the least northeastern thing about me," she agreed, settling into the passenger's seat. "All these years in Massachusetts and New York, and yet I've never gotten used to the winter."

"So, no ice skating tonight," he noted.

Elizabeth froze—figuratively—now. "If that's what you have planned…"

She should have worn a different coat. More practical mittens. Thicker tights under her dress.

"It's not."

"Oh, thank goodness."

One of his low laughs. "This is an indoor activity, I promise."

A dramatic sigh of relief followed. Her own. "Do I get to know where?"

"Soon," he promised. They hadn't turned any music on, so the only sounds that passed between them for a moment were those of the tires, the wind and the intermittent passing cars.

Streets never felt this empty in a city. This intimate.

"I'm sorry about this morning," Mark said, his voice sounding rusty, as if he'd gone days without speaking rather than minutes. "That was just my dad. Nothing to do with you."

Elizabeth swallowed. *Ah.* So, they were acknowledging that awkward breakfast encounter. "I'm sorry. I shouldn't have—"

"Been neighborly? Friendly?"

"Intruded. I shouldn't have intruded."

"Brennan, we were at the most frequented breakfast spot in town. You weren't intruding."

Elizabeth shot him a look he must have read as dubious. Likely because she was.

"It was...nice of you," he added. "To want to say hi."

"Parents usually like me," she confided in a faux whisper to hide how for-real thrown she'd been by the encounter. "I must be losing my touch."

"Trust me. You're not."

Fire in her cheeks again. A flicker. A flame.

"I must have interrupted some kind of conversation then?"

"Sure. Wedding talk. You'd think it was their son getting married. Which just shows how disappointed they must be that it's not." A beat. "Sorry. I shouldn't have said that."

Elizabeth disagreed. "If that's how you feel, you should say it."

There had to be a difference between acknowledging your negative thoughts and indulging them, didn't there? You needed to recognize your feelings in order to seek God's guidance, after all. But she couldn't say that, not without sounding all holier-than-thou and above it all. Which she wasn't. The same insecurities had mired her thoughts all day long.

Mark shrugged. "I just can't win. I'm going to the wedding alone, they're disappointed. I take you, they're—"

He paused.

"Disappointed?" That shouldn't hurt. She barely knew his parents. Why did the apology on his face twist a knife into her stomach?

"Confused. You're Andrew's high school sweetheart. You live in New York."

Indignation swirled in Elizabeth's stomach, hot and almost nauseating. "That isn't fair. I'm not Andrew's... anything. We haven't dated in a long time."

They hadn't *spoken*—really spoken—in a long time.

"Small towns, long memories."

"And your parents don't see the hypocrisy in that? He's marrying your high school sweetheart."

Mark shrugged, staring straight ahead into the dark road.

"I'm sorry." They were talking about his parents. His feelings should take priority, and yet here she was, stuck on her own hurt.

"Why are you sorry?" he asked, incredulous.

"It was my idea, going to the wedding together. If your parents are upset with you about it or giving you a hard time because of it—"

"It wouldn't have been any better if I went alone."

That feverish rush of indignation again. Mark deserved better. More. Unconditional love.

"I'm upsetting you. This isn't how I wanted to start off the night."

"You didn't. You started it off with baked goods. You already won." Before she could chicken out, she asked, "Are your parents always that hard on you?"

She watched Mark's jaw shift. "There's a short and long answer here. But they both start with yes."

Unfair. Unfathomable. "I don't get it. You're smart

and driven and kind and—" she stopped herself from continuing. *Wonderful. One of a kind.*

"I appreciate the pom-poms, Brennan. But I've accepted the relationship I have with my parents. It's okay."

Gratitude for her own parents pulsed through her heart. She might worry about disappointing them, sometimes, but never truly doubted their support.

"That's the short answer," Mark added after a second. "The longer answer is that I don't understand it, either. And it's not okay, really, but it's the way things are."

If she could have hugged him, she would have. Instead, she said, "Have you ever talked to them about it?"

"Not exactly my strong suit."

"Could've fooled me." How far they'd come in a few days.

A small smile. "Enough about my parents. Tell me about your day. Something good."

She didn't want to press the subject of his own family. So she replied, "Well, I went to breakfast with my parents at this place called Daisy's Diner…"

"*After* that."

Elizabeth pushed her hair behind her ears, unsure of whether he'd want to hear about the rest of her day. "I spent the afternoon with Melissa, actually. Tried on my bridesmaid dress again. Talked over coffee."

Mark nodded. "How is she? I heard about her sister. And her harpist. And her wedding planner. Can't be an easy week for her."

"She's stressed, but anyone would be. And you know Melissa—she's sensitive. I'm sure she'll feel better after the wedding. Everything is falling back into place."

Another nod. "That's good."

"She asked about you. She's happy to hear you're doing well, too."

"Good," he repeated. "Good. I am."

He'd gone impenetrable again. She couldn't tell if he was annoyed or ambivalent or okay. Eyes straight on the road. The angles of his face all she could see in the flash of surrounding streetlights.

"It was nice seeing her," Elizabeth rambled on, hoping that if she kept her voice level enough, she could smooth over any blunder. "I told you this the other day, but we haven't felt like friends in a long time—been real enough with each other to be friends. I think we might be getting back there, though."

"That's good to hear." A beat. "I'm using the word *good* a lot, huh?"

"Impress me with your postdoc vocab. How was your day?"

Mark didn't answer for a second. "Oh. You know. Good."

"Mark."

"Sorry, sorry," he said, his lips spreading into a small grin before straightening. "Breakfast, which you saw. A walk. Some job stress, some reading."

"I'd ask how the job searching is going, but I know that's not always a fun question."

Mark took a breath as though about to jump from a great height. Then, "How are you feeling? After last night?"

Elizabeth twisted her hands on her lap. "I'm trying not to think about the rejection, honestly. I'm only home for a few more days. I just want to stay in the moment, enjoy being here with my family and give the rest over to God for now."

All true. Also all easier said than done.

"You haven't told your parents about it?"

"No, they…they've always had so much faith in me. I want to live up to it."

"I don't think that will change because you're having a hard time. Usually, that's when you need faith most."

Elizabeth blinked. Logically, she knew that of course, but emotionally…when it came to people believing in *her*…

"Thank you," she said. "And thank you for staying with me last night. It meant a lot."

"I don't know what you're talking about. I was just there for the Portuguese food," Mark deadpanned. More softly, he added, "Anytime."

They pulled up to a red light. Mark looked over at her, his cool blue eyes arresting hers beneath the street-lights shining through the windshield. Seconds passed.

Elizabeth broke eye contact to look through the car window. She'd forgotten to follow where they were driving, to try to figure out where he was taking her, until they pulled into the parking lot.

"Mermaid Theater?" A small theater between Herons Bay and the Cape. Her parents had taken her here as a kid to watch local and touring productions of their favorite shows. She'd seen *Grease* and *Guys and Dolls* on this stage for the first times, had realized that *Beauty and the Beast* and *Cinderella* weren't just Disney films here. This was where, as a kid with blond pigtails, round cheeks and wide eyes set on the show, she'd fallen in love with the stage. This was where she had decided she wanted to be on it one day.

As a teenager, she'd gotten to perform here. The seniors in Herons Bay's community theater group, the

Cranberry Players, did a show here each year. Elizabeth had felt like a professional actress, a true performer, acting on this stage.

She hadn't been back here in years, except in memory. But here it was in front of her now, just as she remembered—albeit with a few more Christmas lights.

"I know it's not Broadway," Mark said. "But I thought you could use a night at the theater."

The smile that spread across her face didn't strain her lips, didn't feel too cheery or too forced or too anything. Because it was real.

"Mark, this is beyond thoughtful." Horrifyingly, tears welled behind her eyes. How long had it been since she'd visited a theater as a member of the audience? Since her passion for theater had filled her with joy rather than stress and fear?

A hesitant fortifying hand on her shoulder. "Then why do you look like you're about to cry?"

She took a deep breath, forcing the tears back, her smile into place.

"Elizabeth?"

"I'm just happy," she said.

Mark did not look convinced, nor did he remove his palm from her shoulder. Even clad in a sweater dress and wool coat, she swore she could feel its firm strength.

"Does your chin usually waver when you're happy?"

Traitorous chin. Elizabeth was supposed to have better control over her composure than that. Over herself, too.

"Maybe," she said, her voice small. "I really appreciate this, Mark. Ignore the…" She gestured vaguely at herself rather than her articulate her tears.

He studied her face, like she was a thesis. No one ever

looked this hard at her, ever caught that there might be more beneath the surface of her fake-it-till-you-make-it smiles. Her breath seemed to depend upon his next blink.

"As long as you're okay," he said finally.

"I'm okay." She was nostalgic. She was confused. But she was also blessed. "I just miss this."

Mark kept looking at her in that careful, discerning way of his. So steady, as solid as the ice she'd once seen in his gaze. It had thawed now. Hadn't it? When Elizabeth looked at Mark's eyes, all she could see was the sea.

She'd always loved the sea.

"You don't even know what show we're seeing," he said.

"It doesn't matter. I'm just happy to be here." *With you.*

An arched eyebrow. "You don't want to know?"

"I didn't say *that*."

"Let's get inside then," Mark said, only then releasing her shoulder, almost like he'd forgotten he'd put his hand there. Or maybe like he hadn't wanted to let go.

Generally speaking, there were things Mark would rather do than brave the cold New England weather to watch a production of *A Christmas Carol*. Read. Watch a documentary. Visit another favorite hometown restaurant.

Dwell upon the ticking clock of a decision that had been thrust upon him earlier.

Don't think about that. Not now. Not here. Not with her next to you. He couldn't trust himself to remain objective.

Was there anything he'd rather do tonight than sit with Elizabeth, just as he was right now? No. She glowed next to him in their orchestra seats, her eyes shining, and not with tears anymore. He gave a silent prayer of thanks for that.

While Scrooge reckoned with the Ghost of Christmas Past, Mark kept glancing over at Elizabeth. His attention was bound to her as to a clock's pendulum, swinging back to her profile again and again. Inevitably.

What would he have made of the Mermaid Theater if he'd walked in alone? He'd come here as a kid with his family and mostly recalled impatience that he couldn't read the next chapter of his book until the cast's final bows. But he'd been young. Maybe, even without Eliza-beth, he would have seen the beauty of the theater now. The rustic New England charm of the building's exterior with its gray shingles and striped awning. And then, inside, the wavy-haired mermaids painted on the walls. Before them, on the stage, Charles Dickens's story, which was over a century old, unfurled.

He didn't think Elizabeth had ever acted in this play. At least not in high school. Since Melissa had always done tech for those shows, he'd dutifully attended each one with Andrew—*Into the Woods* and *Seussical* and *Beauty and the Beast* and *The Sound of Music*. But the Herons Bay Community Center's theater had hosted those performances.

Elizabeth and Melissa had done a show here with their community theater group the summer after high school graduation, he recalled. It had been a big deal, something they'd looked forward to for years. With his breakup with Melissa still so fresh, he'd felt too awkward to attend. He regretted that now. He would have liked to have seen Elizabeth on this stage in whatever role she'd taken on.

A hand on his wrist, soft and lavender-scented, pulled him back into the moment.

Thank you, Elizabeth mouthed at him as the scene ended, her attention turned back on him for a moment.

Mark didn't need to find an answer, because the show was already resuming. Her hand was gone. Dramatic voices as loud as the stage lights. Elizabeth rapt and absorbed once more. Mark's heart throbbed.

This had been a bad idea.

He'd received a call from the English Literature department at a university in Chicago he'd interviewed with last spring. It was among the universities he'd applied to again this year. Apparently, one of their professors had run into a family emergency that would prevent him from coming back from the winter break, so they needed someone to start right at the beginning of next semester. His doctoral advisor had a connection there and had spoken up on his behalf. Now he somehow had an impossible opportunity: a temporary position, out of nowhere, which might lead to more. In a few weeks, he could have classes to take over, a curriculum to teach, a prestigious university's reputation behind his research.

Everything he'd always wanted. So, why hadn't he given an immediate yes? Why, when he thought about accepting the offer, moving to Chicago, leaving Herons Bay behind once and for all, did his heart throb?

His eyes betrayed him again. Elizabeth filled his vision once more. A woman he wasn't supposed to want. Who was returning to New York in less than a week. Who had the potential to hurt him, much more than his parents, if anything real took root between them.

This was for the best, a sign from God not to let things progress further. He couldn't turn this position down even if he wanted to. Academia was too cutthroat, opportunities like this one too few and far between. He'd be shooting his career in the foot. His future.

Onstage, the Ghost of Christmas Present entered the scene. A good reminder for him. Stay in the present. He didn't need to leave yet.

Mark did his best to take in the show. It seemed well acted, well produced, at least to his admittedly novice eye. This was the first production of *A Christmas Carol* he'd seen onstage, so he couldn't exactly compare and contrast.

Elizabeth could, though.

"I owe you," she said to him at intermission. "So much. This is wonderful."

Mark shifted in his seat. "It's not that big of a deal."

"It is to me."

She beamed at him, and Mark couldn't believe that just a few days ago, he might not have seen the difference between this expression and her show smile. Her every emotion etched itself across her face now: excitement, gratitude, affection, joy.

For the musical, he reminded himself, not for him.

Quiet persisted long enough that he assumed her thoughts had drifted to new subjects. But then, when he was about to ask if she wanted Swedish Fish or M&M's from the concession stand, she added, "You're a really good man, Mark Hayes. I can't believe that I went so many years without realizing that, but I feel so blessed that we found each other again."

"And by *found each other*, you mean Facebook-messaging me out of the blue to grab coffee so you could ask me a on a fake date."

"Obviously, yes."

The moment of levity took the conversation onto easier ground. But Mark realized he should have given a more earnest reply—should have told her how blessed he felt to have gotten to know her, too. How conflicted he was that whatever spark had flared between them wouldn't have the chance to ignite.

Over intermission, Elizabeth headed to the concessions line. Treating Mark with snacks was the least she could do since he refused to tell her how much their tickets had cost *or* let her pay him back.

Stubborn. Generous. Kind.

Elizabeth considered the display case of candy. She was debating whether pretzels might suit Mark better than sweets when a voice cracked her concentration.

"Elizabeth Brennan?"

She turned around. She recognized that voice, didn't she?

"Oh, my gosh," she said. "Cecelia!"

Behind her in line stood the director of the Cranberry Players, her old community theater group. The woman who had encouraged her to pursue theater, who had taught her so much about the art of acting. She looked just the same, though Elizabeth hadn't seen her in years. Dark hair, as long and wavy as that of the mermaids painted on the wall. A long swaying silver dress—the bohemian sort she'd always worn. Christmas-red lipstick. Pine tree earrings dangling from her lobes to complete the look.

"I hoped that was you! I couldn't see your face, but I'd recognize the back of that head anywhere."

Elizabeth wrapped her arms around the older woman in a hug. Same rose perfume she remembered. Being back in this theater, seeing this face from her past, it was like she'd fallen down the rabbit hole and into a memory.

"I feel like I haven't seen you in ages," Elizabeth said. "How have you been?"

"That's what happens when you move to New York," Cecelia said with a laugh. "Enjoying the city?"

Her standard answer was on the tip of her tongue. If there was ever a woman to impress, ever a role model to hide her insecurities from...

"That hard, huh?"

Elizabeth pushed her hair behind her ears and settled on "It's nice being home this week."

"A diplomatic answer if I've ever heard one. I followed my dreams to New York, too, remember. It was a while back ago now, mind you, but it feels like yesterday. The brutal open calls, the high hopes, the bitter disappointments, the excitement, the exhaustion..."

Frozen. She felt frozen, caught in stasis. Was she so transparent? Did she look as worn down as she felt? What had happened to her performer's composure?

"Oh, I wouldn't have traded that time for anything," Cecelia went on. "But there's a reason I moved to Herons Bay and started the Cranberry Players. A friend got me a summer job at a nearby arts camp—closed now, sadly—and I couldn't bear to go back to the city. And then I met my Harry here, of course. You know the rest."

Elizabeth swallowed. There were questions she wanted to ask, but the line before her was dwindling, her turn to overpay for candy approaching. Did Cecelia regret leaving the city without making it on Broadway? Did she wonder what would have happened if she'd stayed? And why had she stoked Elizabeth's dreams so much if her years in New York had been anything but dreamy?

"You never answered," she said, rallying. "How have you and Harry been doing lately?"

A frown weighed on Cecelia's red lips. "This isn't public knowledge yet, but it will be soon, so I might as well tell you. We're moving to Florida in a few months. My mom is all alone down there, and Harry has been wanting warmer weather. We'd be there now, for Christmas, but I wanted one last holiday in Herons Bay. And to attend Melissa's wedding, of course."

That did it. Elizabeth's practiced smile, her careful composure, faltered. "What about the Cranberry Players?"

"It breaks my heart, but I haven't found anyone to take it over. It's just been me ever since Jill—" her cofounder, another mentor from Elizabeth's past "—turned snowbird."

Hardly knowing what she was doing, Elizabeth pulled her into another hug. "I'm so sorry, Cecelia. Not about the move—I'm sure Florida will be lovely. But…" Her theater company. Her legacy. The role she'd played in Herons Bay all these years, nurturing young actors. All gone?

A gentle pat on her back. "Oh, it's all in God's plan. New doors, new opportunities. He's been nudging me to move on for a while now, I think. But I'm stubborn, as I'm sure you remember. I hoped I'd find a replacement before I left, someone like you, who I've worked with and trust. Someone who lives and breathes theater."

Those words did something funny to her chest. Something fluttery.

"Thank you," Elizabeth said before biting her lip.

Would she have a chance to speak privately to Cecelia at Melissa's wedding? She'd assume so, but just in case...

"It means a lot to run into you here tonight. To see you again before you move. The Cranberry Players did so much for me. I wouldn't still be acting if not for you."

"Don't make me teary, Elizabeth Brennan. This mascara isn't waterproof. Now, I'm sure you're busy with your family, but stop by my house anytime this week. And I'll see you at the wedding, of course."

"Of course," Elizabeth echoed.

"How is Melissa doing with the big day so close?"

"You remember Melissa."

"Stressed?"

"Very," she said. Maybe this wasn't her business to share, but the news that Herons Bay would soon lose their main source of community theater must have knocked the caution from her tongue. And besides, Cecelia had watched Melissa grow up, had been a mentor for her, too. "There have been a few...surprises. Flight delays, wedding cake mishaps, an injured harpist. We've solved most of them, but that last one is tough."

A slow smile stole over Cecelia's features. "Elizabeth, I might just have a solution for you."

Elizabeth listened wide-eyed as Cecelia informed her that the harp was one of the several instruments in her repertoire. And Elizabeth couldn't believe it, but she would be pleased to play at Melissa's wedding.

"Are you sure?" Elizabeth asked, even as her heart soared. "Melissa invited you as a guest."

Cecelia waved a dismissive hand. "I love performing, and I've always adored you girls. I'll call Melissa tomorrow to arrange it."

Elizabeth couldn't help but throw her arms around Cecelia again in a flash of a hug. A three-hug conversation. A little much? Possibly. Merited? Each and every one.

"Thank you. Thank you, thank you, thank you. Melissa will be so thrilled."

"She got us through enough behind-the-scenes mishaps back when you two were in high school. I'm happy to do the same for her." A sniff belied her smile. "Between the two of us, I think this will be the perfect farewell to Herons Bay—performing for the entire town."

Elizabeth offered a silent prayer of gratitude to God. As long as Phoebe's flight landed on time tomorrow, Melissa's wedding would be on course once more. Smooth sailing ahead.

God clearly had a plan for Melissa. Elizabeth had to trust He did for her as well.

After the show, after most of the audience had cleared from the theater, Elizabeth asked Mark if they could linger. Just for another minute.

"I have nowhere to be," he said, leaning against one of the mermaid-decorated walls.

Feeling a little silly, a little sad, Elizabeth took in the empty stage. The audience's applause as the cast took final bows seemed to echo through the room still.

"I haven't been to a show in forever," she heard herself say softly.

"I can't believe that."

"I audition for plenty. And I've had minor roles here and there. But I usually don't have the money for tickets or the time to wait in the day-of discounted line. This has been wonderful, Mark."

Ironic that she'd moved to New York to devote her life to acting but had found more joy helping a couple of kids put on a little play two nights ago and in watching a local theater production tonight than New York had brought her in years now. She lived in a city known for its arts scene, but she'd become so obsessed with joining it that she rarely got to enjoy it.

Cecelia's words itched at her mind. The Cranberry Players had brought her a lot of happiness once upon a time.

Mark gave a stiff, uncomfortable nod—his go-to when faced with praise or gratitude, she'd noticed. "Well, it's Christmas. And I still owed you for that worry shell."

As they made their way into the hall, following the last of the audience out the front doors, Elizabeth laughed. "This way outdoes a shell from the beach."

"I don't know. It's a great shell," he said, pulling it from his pocket. *He kept it.* Her heart grew a size.

"Seriously, Mark. This was huge," she said. "I'm sure you noticed last night… I've been reconsidering things. Career-wise. Sometimes, I feel like Captain Ahab chasing a white whale, though I still haven't actually read more than a few pages of *Moby Dick*, so tell me if that doesn't make sense."

"It does. And you're not."

He sounded so certain. So sure of her. Elizabeth wanted to wrap those words around herself like a scarf, to warm her when doubt beckoned. But of course, she couldn't. They only had a few more days together before the holidays ended and reality called.

"Thank you," she said again, teeth just then starting to chatter as they exited the theater. Speaking of scarves, she adjusted hers to better block out the cold. Elizabeth lifted her gaze for one last look at Mermaid Theater, its familiarity, its hope, its echo of her past.

That was when she noticed the mistletoe hanging above their heads.

Elizabeth's heart pounded. Her teeth stopped chattering; heat rushed to her cheeks. There were countless reasons not to kiss Mark Hayes. Only, with that mistletoe still claiming the corner of her vision, she couldn't think of one.

"Nothing to thank me for," Mark said.

She had myriad replies for that, too, but didn't say any of them. Instead, Elizabeth closed her eyes and grazed her mouth against his. Shy. Careful. Cautious. But then his lips moved against hers, firm and seeking, and Elizabeth felt herself rising to her tiptoes to wrap her arms around his neck. She let herself fall into that kiss and every sensation that came with it.

She hadn't kissed anyone in a very long time. The last time had been onstage—just a peck, just a minor role. Nothing like this. Nothing real.

From a distance, Mark was all angles and sharp edges. But right now, his chin prodded hers so softly. His hands latched so gently onto her cheeks. Elizabeth certainly wasn't thinking about the cold anymore. She was thinking about how solid he was against her, how cherished she felt in his arms, how she wanted this moment to go on forever...

Nevertheless, she broke away for a breath, leaning her forehead against his.

"Was that okay?" she breathed.

He blinked. He staggered back. And then his eyes frosted over. She watched it happen—his face going hard again, his hands dropping to his sides. He took another step back, leaving her standing there, hiked onto her tiptoes, cheeks flaming for a new reason. Her heart dropped along with her heels back to the ground. Maybe he thought she'd only kissed him because of the mistletoe. Safest to let him think so. Easiest to tell herself that was the only reason. Not truthful, though. She could be honest. Brave.

"This night has been really special," she said, voice hoarse. "The last few days have. I know our date to this wedding wasn't supposed to be real, but…maybe it could be?"

Silence. Mark looked too tense for words. For movement. For anything. Where was the man who had just held her, kissed her, as though he might really care for her? Had it all been in her head?

"I can't." A long pause. "Elizabeth—"

Not *Brennan*. One by one, the butterflies that had buoyed her stomach fell to a heap of dread in her gut.

"I'm sorry," she said, backing away. "I'm so sorry. I misread things. That was completely inappropriate. Can you forget that happened? Please?"

What else was there to say? However much he'd seemed to enjoy the kiss in the moment, however many times she'd felt his eyes on her through the show tonight, however she felt about him…

"Elizabeth," he tried again.

But she was already fleeing to his parked car. Debating checking her Uber app for an alternate ride home. Wishing she'd never spotted that mistletoe, never put her feelings on the line.

Hadn't she learned by now? When she wanted something, when she went for something, she'd fail. Every time.

Chapter Eleven

Elizabeth Brennan had kissed him last night. Confessed feelings for him, which he felt echoed in his own heart. And he'd crushed her.

That was all Mark could think about as he looked over the official offer letter that had reached his inbox this morning. A teaching position at a university, if only for a semester to start. He should be reading it word by word, again and again, savoring the win. The accomplishment. The realization of years and years of hard work. But all he could think about was the hope that had flared in Elizabeth's sea-glass eyes when she'd pressed her lips against his...and how he'd shattered it. How *right* she'd felt in his arms, though she didn't belong there.

Eventually, she'd realize that. Change her mind. Choose someone else. He had to be practical and take the offer he could trust. How could he know that the other applications he'd sent would yield results this time, when they hadn't before?

The drive home last night had been awkward, him looking for the words to explain, her pretending nothing had happened. When he dropped her at her parents' house, he'd thought about walking her to the door. But instead he'd let her go. Watched her walk away from him.

He was hiding in the back of Blue Heron Books today, where he'd often lost himself growing up. Interspersed between all the shelves, out of the way, sat a few leather armchairs. The owners of the store, Annie and Alex Anderson, never minded if their customers sat down and paged through a book for an hour. In return, they'd garnered a great deal of loyalty—his included. Even Mark's favorite bookstores in New York lacked this kind of sitting area. The implication in those stores was clear: browse, buy and leave. Herons Bay wasn't like that. Age had made Mark appreciate that more.

"Tea?"

He looked up at the sound of Alex's jovial voice. The store owner's familiar face had just a few more wrinkles than it had when Mark had worked here in high school. Otherwise, he looked just the same. Salt-and-pepper hair, thick glasses on his nose, a cable-knit sweater. Currently, Alex was making his way to him through the sundry shelves, a platter in hand. It held a teapot decorated with swirling calligraphy and a mug.

The past few days had reminded Mark that there were things he loved in Herons Bay: the candy-making at Sweet Somethings. The picturesque walks and drives. The food at Sousa's. And this bookstore. So why, suddenly, was Elizabeth's face—so hopeful, then so hurt, then so unreadable in that performer's composure of hers—flaring through his thoughts again?

"Please," Mark said thankfully, resisting the urge to refuse out of politeness. Annie and Alex had been offering their customers hot tea during the winter months for as long as he could remember. They wouldn't keep it up if they didn't want people to accept.

Unburdening Alex of the tray, Mark set it down on the table between the armchairs.

The older man poured Mark's cup, then another for himself before joining him. "Let me see what you've found today," he said. "You've always had good taste."

"You've always had a great selection," Mark countered, taking his mug in hand.

As Alex flipped through his finds—a mythological retelling, a nonfiction title about nineteenth-century American writers, an anthology of short fiction—Mark wondered, with a pang, whether he should bother to buy these books. If he really was moving to Chicago, he'd have other things to fill his time before the semester started: finding an apartment, moving his things there, familiarizing himself with the curriculums he'd be taking over. Starting over.

"All good picks," Alex concluded.

"All your picks," Mark said, a half smile burgeoning through his stress. Toward the end of December, Alex and Annie always arranged a table of their favorite releases from that year. Mark had learned to trust them.

"Exactly," he said. Standing up, he patted him on the shoulder. "Welcome home, Mark." He walked back the way he'd come.

For once, Mark didn't want to counter that he wasn't *back home*—not really, not officially, not forever. Right now, the thought of leaving wrung at him. More than he'd expected. For better or worse, he knew Herons Bay, knew the people here, and they knew him. He couldn't say the same for Chicago. Excitement should ensue when he thought about starting over there, but Mark couldn't see beyond the loneliness stretching before him.

When he first heard someone walking through the stacks, he didn't think much of it. Not until he heard a soft, "Oh."

He looked up to find Elizabeth frozen before him with her fingers on the spine of a shelved book.

Mark stood. Then wondered why he'd stood. Then wondered when he could comfortably sit back down without making things any more awkward.

Elizabeth dropped her hand from the shelf, book abandoned or forgotten. "Hi, I probably should have expected to run into you here."

It hurt that she didn't sound happy about that, that her eyes were darting for the closest exit. But what else could he expect? He had tried to apologize, wanted to explain on the drive home last night, but she'd shut down. She'd gone back into that actress mode of hers he'd never known what to do with, pretending everything was shiny and bright. Brushing off any effort at apology he made.

"It's a small town," he agreed finally. He was still standing. As if he'd chase her if she left—which would be ridiculous and inappropriate and better suited to an early 2000s rom-com than to his life. This wasn't a romantic comedy.

"Right." A breath. She smoothed her silken hair behind her ear. "Well, I better…"

She had just started to leave when Mark managed to say, "Brennan, come on. We're going to the rehearsal dinner together tonight."

"I know," she said, crossing her arms at her chest.

So, couldn't she just sit down? Couldn't they return to the ease they'd had together these last few days?

"So, you're going to need to talk to me again at some point," he settled for replying.

"We're fine, Mark. Don't worry." Distant. Aloof. Unreadable and untouchable. No. They weren't fine.

"Last night, I didn't explain…"

"There's no need." Her eyes darted around the room again, this time at the other customers who were starting to look at them curiously. "It's really fine, Mark. Enjoy the books. I'll see you tonight."

He was still on his feet when she walked away. If he were the hero of a romantic comedy, he would do something useful. Run after her. Fix this.

Mark lowered himself back into his armchair. What was the point? If he accepted this position, he'd be moving to Chicago. He took a sip from his mug, which he could barely taste even though Annie and Alex had a great selection of teas. And then he opened a book and stared at its words without processing them.

Like Elizabeth had said, everything was fine.

Elizabeth was at a loss. For a lot of reasons, many of which were best ignored. But when it came to tomorrow's wedding…

Melissa should, by all accounts, have looked happy now. Phoebe had made it home this morning. Kristen was doing a beautiful job with her cake. And true to her word, Cecelia had given Melissa a call this morning and was now set to play the harp at her wedding. Every hiccup scared away. Calm waters now, just in time for tonight's rehearsal dinner.

Still, when Melissa stopped by the B&B and asked if Elizabeth wanted to take a walk with her, she hadn't seemed triumphant or reassured or unburdened. Tension still lined her forehead, pulled at her mouth. Worry still squirmed through her eyes. Even Mary Tyler Morkie's tail-wagging attentions weren't enough to dispel them.

The three of them walked along Water Street now, MTM leading the way.

"I still can't believe you have a dog," Melissa said, staring at the little ball of fur Elizabeth had bundled into a plaid jacket.

"Melissa. You didn't come by to talk about my dog. Did something else happen?"

Wrapping her arms around herself as they walked, Melissa shook her head. "Everything is perfect."

Then why were her nails nibbled rather than manicured? Why did she sound so full of dread, the way Elizabeth felt when she recollected yesterday evening? A kiss—what should have been a beautiful romantic moment—had made Mark shut down again. As though she were a stranger or, worse, an object of pity. She'd put her feelings on the line, and he'd made it clear he didn't share them. For all the rejection she'd faced lately, his stung the most.

Best not to dwell on that.

"Exactly. Tomorrow, you're going to marry the man you love, with your sister and a harpist and a wedding cake all in attendance. And then you'll fly off to wherever it is you're honeymooning and put all the wedding stress behind you. Like you said. Perfect."

Melissa was twisting her hair again. "You're right. You're right."

If only she sounded as though she believed it. Could Cecelia's news about the Cranberry Players have upset her like this?

"It was surreal seeing Cecelia last night out of the blue. Did she tell you—"

"That she's moving? That the Cranberry Players have done their last show?" Melissa sniffled. "I can't believe it."

Neither could Elizabeth. To the point that she'd actually begun to wonder… What if God wanted her try a new path? This path? What if all her striving in New York had been leading her back here, preparing her to do for this generation's teens what Cecelia had done for her? The road ahead would prove a challenge without a partner to share the work and responsibility with her, but nothing Elizabeth had done as an adult had felt particularly easy.

"It breaks my heart," Elizabeth said. In more ways than one. How could she abandon the life she'd built in New York? All the auditions, all the heartache, all the hope? "Is that why you seem down?"

Mary Tyler Morkie slowed down to sniff a nearby bush. Elizabeth took that opportunity to stop and really look at Melissa. Seize eye contact. Solve for y.

"What do you mean?" Melissa asked, her voice wavering an octave.

"Nothing is wrong with the wedding. Why are you still this stressed?"

A nervous glance around the road as if seeking reassurance that they were alone. Other than a car reversing out of its driveway, then veering in the other direction, there wasn't another soul to be seen. Melissa hemmed one breath, then hawed another.

Mary Tyler Morkie guided them ahead. Once they started moving again, Melissa finally spoke.

"I'm not sure Andrew wants to get married."

The confession came as a whisper, so wobbly that it took Elizabeth a moment to decipher it. Once she did, white noise descended upon her brain. "What?"

Melissa took longer, faster strides, as if trying to out-pace her own words.

For once, the cold winter breeze made for a pleasant distraction as it whipped her hair against her cheeks. Melissa didn't think Andrew wanted to marry her? A day before they were due to say their vows?

"I know what you're going to say. Of course Andrew wants to marry me. He asked me to marry him. I've spent the past year planning our wedding."

Elizabeth pasted her lips together, swallowing those exact replies.

"But he's been so distant lately. And I wanted to talk to Phoebe about it when she got home, because I was never brave enough to bring it up over the phone to her. Only, her arrival kept getting pushed, and now that she's here, she can barely keep her eyes open. And I've been wanting to talk to you about it, but it's uncomfortable with the history."

Elizabeth was so tired of that history. Worrying about it and the optics of attending her ex's wedding alone versus with his cousin. Letting it tarnish her friendship with Melissa. The version of herself who had dated Andrew Hayes didn't even exist anymore. The person she was now needed to release old fears and hurts. Even if Mark didn't have feelings for her, at least she'd opened her heart—and survived it. That meant she could do it again someday.

"I can't talk to my mom," Melissa continued, pulling Elizabeth from her thoughts. "She's so excited. And all my other friends are also Andrew's friends…"

"What about Andrew?" Elizabeth said as they turned onto a ghost street—most of the houses on this particular road belonged to summer people and snowbirds. "Isn't this something you should talk to him about?"

"No," Melissa said, panting for reasons that clearly had nothing to do with their walk. Her breath lingered visibly in the cool air. "No."

"Melissa, I've barely seen Andrew in years. I can't offer any insight here."

"But you used to know him so well. You were his first love. That has to count for something."

Did it? All four of them were different people now. Life had pulled them in various directions. Somehow, hers had pulled her toward Mark. With a deep breath, Elizabeth said, "Can we back up a bit? Why don't you think he wants to go through with the wedding?"

Melissa's reply burst from her lips as from a dam. "Andrew has always been the perfect boyfriend. Attentive and sweet and romantic. But he's been so preoccupied lately. Like he was...you know, before you broke up."

Elizabeth recalled. The cheerful armor he'd donned to cover up the problems in their relationship. She had her own suit of it.

"That was different. Haven't you been preoccupied, too? You've both been planning a wedding."

Melissa shook her head. "*I've* been planning a wedding. All Andrew has done is approve the color scheme and the flowers and contribute half the guest list. I haven't left anything for him to stress over."

"It's a huge day. A huge change. Maybe he's worried about not knowing how to be a good enough husband for you or...I don't know, something with his students or his art. Don't tell yourself stories, Melissa. They might not be true."

Was that what Elizabeth was doing? Telling herself a story without giving its feature character a voice? Not allowing Mark to explain himself the night before, closing off any attempt at an honest conversation with the same armor Andrew used? Though she wanted to put their history behind her, she couldn't deny that they'd learned a lot about relationships with each other—both good and bad.

"I've been trying not to," Melissa said, voice breaking. "I've been trying this whole time."

A soon-to-be bride shouldn't look like Melissa did right now, her face so lined with sadness, her eyes so wide with fears.

"Will you talk to him for me?" Melissa asked. "Please?"

"Me?"

"I've never been any good at confrontation. Neither of us have. You know that."

All the more reason to communicate that before the wedding.

"You need to have this conversation with him," Elizabeth said. This wasn't fair to her. Wedding guest or not, bridesmaid or not, she didn't belong center stage in this drama.

"I don't know how. Every time, I freeze. I'm so scared he's going to break my heart."

This wasn't her place. This wasn't fair.

"Why me?" Elizabeth asked again. Why not Jenna, their mutual friend from college? Why not her parents? Why not Andrew's parents? Why not anyone else in Herons Bay?

"Who else?"

Casting her gaze to the cloudy sky, praying for guidance, Elizabeth said, "You're about to vow to spend the rest of your lives together. I think you should talk to him yourself," Elizabeth said. She didn't want to sound harsh, but how didn't Melissa realize the solution here? And that recruiting her didn't factor into it? That marriage would require Melissa to confront her husband at times like these? That Elizabeth hadn't known how to do so back in the day, either, so what made her think she could now?

"Elle, please. I know myself. I won't do it. And I know him—he wouldn't tell me the truth, not if he thought it would hurt me. But he might tell you. I can't spend the rest of my life worrying that my husband never really wanted to marry me."

To avoid spinning around another conversational circle, Elizabeth held her tongue. Once again, she had no room to throw stones. Wasn't she doing the same to Mark on a smaller scale? Avoiding him. And her reasons weren't any better than Melissa's. Fear. Humiliation. Bruised pride.

"Tell Andrew that I'll stop by—quickly—after the rehearsal dinner."

"I will," Melissa said, her words racing each other. "Thank you. Thank you, thank you, thank you."

Elizabeth gave another silent prayer for help.

Chapter Twelve

In the hours leading up to the rehearsal dinner, Mark received a text from Andrew asking if he wanted to go on a jog together. Like old times.

Sure, he texted back. Let me know where.

As much as he wanted to hide in Blue Heron Books all day with a stack of paperbacks and a cup of tea, a jog would get his mind moving. His thoughts off Elizabeth. His heart back in alignment with the job that would begin all his dreams.

Not to mention, Andrew hadn't reached out to him like this in a long time. And who knew when they'd have another chance to catch up? Andrew would get married tomorrow, leave on his ski mountain honeymoon soon after, and then Mark would move to Chicago.

Besides, one didn't turn down the very olive branch he'd been hoping for.

"Thanks for doing this," Andrew panted now as the two of them ran down the Cape Cod Canal bikeway, beneath the Bourne Bridge. "I know it's not the best weather."

During the summer months, they'd share this seven-mile stretch with cyclists and power walkers and strollers. Apparently, though, most people had more sense than to run right by the water in December.

"As long as you don't get pneumonia the day before your wedding," Mark replied.

"That would give new meaning to 'cold feet,' huh?"

If Mark weren't breathing so hard, he might have laughed. As it was, he grunted a sound that might have been laughter. From the pace they were keeping, he'd swear that Andrew was trying to outrun his thoughts, too.

They ran in companionable silence for a while after that, each plugged into his own workout music. Between the waterfront wind and their unrelenting pace, a conversation didn't seem on the table. Which was fine. What did they have to talk about anyway? Their respective exes?

At the mile two marker painted onto the pavement, Andrew tapped his arm. Mark paused his running playlist.

"Turn around?" he asked.

Mark nodded. That was the thing about the canal walkway, it went straight, not circular. You had to commit to trekking back exactly as far as you went forward. In some ways, that was how Mark had felt this past month living at home. Like he'd reached a finish line, a landmark achievement of his adult life, only to walk straight back into his teenage shoes. Another reason he had to take the offered position.

Without discussing it, they slowed their pace on the way back. Mark had no problem with that. He hadn't run much this week and hadn't been expecting a four-mile jaunt today.

"It's great running with you again," Andrew said. "No one pushes me like you do."

Mark let out another laugh-grunt. "I think you have that switched around."

This whole run, he'd been kicking up his pace notch by notch, determined to keep a step ahead of Andrew. He'd accepted that his cousin would always outpace him at plenty. Fine. But not running.

"I've been trying to keep up with you this whole time, man," Andrew said. "Are we running from someone I don't know about?"

The email in his inbox awaiting a reply. The hurt on Elizabeth's heart-shaped face.

"I could say the same to you."

"Touché," Andrew said with a shrug, pulling a water bottle out of the pack on his back and pouring its contents down his throat. "I wanted to thank you again for standing up at my wedding. I know it all got messed up, that I messed it up by not asking earlier, but it means a lot."

Mark's turn to shrug. "You're my cousin."

"Yeah."

Their sneakers pounded on the ground, filling the quiet that itched between them. Andrew had made an effort, so Mark coughed and asked, "Everything all set with the wedding now?"

A nod of Andrew's head. "I'm sure you heard some of the drama from your parents and Elizabeth. But everything seems on track now, God willing. You have no idea how much stress I've been under."

Hard to say whether it was exertion or something more that lurked between the letters of Andrew's answer. But he didn't sound convinced.

"Hard to believe, huh?" he continued. "Melissa and I getting married, you bringing Elizabeth as your date.

Sometimes, high school feels like a minute ago. And sometimes, it really doesn't."

"You're talking to a man who had to move back in with his parents. I get it."

Andrew winced. "I'm sorry I didn't reach out sooner. Things have been tough with the wedding, with trying to figure out what comes after. But I should have been there for you when you moved home. I know—well, I know what your dad is like. I thought maybe I'd make things worse between you two."

Mark almost tripped over his own sneakers.

"Nothing against him," Andrew said quickly. "He's a great uncle. But he's always been hard on you."

And easy on Andrew. And Mark had never been able to figure out *why*. Was it just that he had less in common with his dad than his cousin did? Or was it more than that, something deeper-seated within Mark that his dad took issue with? Something lesser in him? Something that made him less worthy of his love?

"I didn't know—"

"That I'd noticed? Come on."

"You never said anything."

Now color overtook his cousin's face—more color, that was. With Andrew's fair complexion, running had already turned his cheeks ruddy. "I should have. It always made me uncomfortable growing up, but I didn't know how to broach it."

Fair enough. What could Andrew have said back then? Mark had never brought it up, either.

"You know, it's only because I'm not his son," Andrew said now. "It's a different dynamic."

And because Mark wasn't steadily employed or as

friendly or as knowledgeable about Boston sports or insert lacking here.

"But you're a big-city hotshot with a PhD. Even he must admit that."

"Ha." Mark didn't realize for a moment that he'd vocalized that noise.

"Really?"

"I don't have a job, Drew." The way his dad had looked at him when he'd admitted that he hadn't found a position last spring, after his first round of academic job searching. It had reflected the shriveling of Mark's self-confidence, his wrecked plans. All the more reason to grab on to this opportunity in Chicago with both hands. No matter how much he'd prefer one of the positions he'd applied for in New England or New York.

"That's a matter of time. You get to go by Dr. Hayes."

"I'm almost thirty, unemployed, living at home and single. The rest doesn't mean much to him."

Andrew heaved a breath to catch up with him. When had Mark started running again? Which failure was he outrunning now?

"He must be happy you're taking Elizabeth to the wedding, then."

"Nope."

"No? I thought he liked her."

When you were dating her. "It is what it is. I don't know why I expected differently."

"I'm sorry, man. Elizabeth is a great girl. He'll come around."

Andrew sounded so sincere. So concerned for him. So invested in a relationship of convenience that Mark had ruined overnight.

"It's not like that. We're not—" anything, real, talking right now "—serious."

Andrew paused, seemingly for the sole purpose of raising an eyebrow at him. "Didn't you take her to a play last night?"

"Men can like theater."

"Sure. Men can. I do. You do not. Enough said there."

Sometimes, Mark felt so alone, so unknowable, that he forgot how well his cousin used to know him. How well he still did in some ways.

"You don't feel strange about it?"

"Because you're dating my ex-girlfriend of ten years ago? Pot. Kettle."

That was what he had been reassuring his dad all week. Still, he'd wondered if Andrew might hold it against him, never mind the hypocrisy. He should have known better. For as long as he could remember, Andrew had been kind, fair, beloved by all for a reason. When had he built his cousin into a villain? After Melissa? Before? Had their friendship suffered under the weight of his father's criticism?

"I never asked you how you felt about Melissa and me," Andrew said after a moment. "That's why I didn't ask you to be a groomsman earlier. I thought you might still hold that against me. I guess when I heard about you and Elizabeth, I figured maybe you understood." His cousin held up both hands, even as he started jogging again. "Not that it's the same."

"I don't hold it against you," Mark said. It hadn't made things easier with his dad, the apparent proof that even his high school girlfriend preferred his cousin. But that wasn't Andrew's fault. He'd let his dad's issues mar their relationship for too long. All his relationships.

Andrew slowed. "Thank you. Seriously, Mark. For the record, I really am happy for you and Elizabeth. She deserves someone like you."

Mark swallowed. That meant more than Andrew could possibly know, but... "It can't go anywhere."

"Why not?"

He hadn't told anyone yet, had hoarded this information to himself like dragon's gold. Saying it aloud would make it real. Would open him up to comments and critiques he wasn't ready for.

"It would be pretty long distance. I was offered a job in Chicago yesterday. At a university."

Andrew halted. Mark had no choice but to do the same. "In an English Department?"

"It's temporary. But it could lead to something permanent."

Without meaning to, he thought of Elizabeth again.

Andrew wrapped his arms around him, clapping him on the back. They untangled quickly when the cold sweat on both their arms registered. "Mark, that's awesome. Congratulations."

"Thank you." The genuine joy in Andrew's voice surprised him, but why should it? His cousin rallied his own spirits. It *was* awesome. Things like this didn't happen. "I'd appreciate it if you didn't mention it to the family. I haven't told anyone else yet."

If only he could count on this same reaction from his dad. Sad that they'd reached a point where he didn't want to share his achievements with his family for fear of them being diminished. He could picture plenty of reactions from his dad—*About time, eh, son? Shame you couldn't find anything in the Northeast. What's the pay?*—and would prefer not to deal with a single one of them. He was already fighting off those same doubts.

Andrew peered over at him as they started jogging once more. "Why not? You don't think they'd be happy for you?"

Mark shrugged. How did one vocalize the thoughts he was having? *My parents don't have the best track record for celebrating my achievements.* Not to mention: *For some reason, I'm not excited to accept my dream job.*

"For what it's worth, I think they will be. But if they aren't, you know there's always your other parent."

Mark raised a brow.

"Your Heavenly Father. Feel free to steal that for a class lecture."

"I will not be doing that."

"Fair enough."

Easier to fall into banter than soul-searing examinations of his relationship with his parents. But Andrew's corny words kept churning in his brain. Why did he keep looking for validation in earthly places like so many of the doomed heroes of the classics he studied? Why couldn't he trust that God loved him unconditionally? He'd ignored the discomfort he'd felt pushing Elizabeth away last night, telling himself the right thing didn't always come easily. But had he really been ignoring his intuition? The voice of the Holy Spirit? Was he choosing the wrong fork in the road?

Mark's head hurt. He kept running.

"Have you accepted yet?" Andrew said, restoring the conversation to easier ground. What *should* have been easier ground. Mark hadn't yet and he couldn't say why. If he was getting what he'd always wanted, why was he stalling?

"Soon," he said. "It would be stupid to refuse it. You know how the job search went for me last year. I might not get another opportunity like this."

Academia was competitive. There were only so many positions like this one available and so many more intelligent, skilled applicants vying for each one.

"I get it," Andrew said, the corners of his mouth turning down. "Don't get me wrong, I'll be bummed if you leave. I was hoping to reconnect more after the wedding. But it's your future."

Exactly. If only honey-blond hair and hummed show tunes didn't keep unraveling his thoughts. *Sunshine*, his mom had called her. But why did she assume he'd get burned in the end? Didn't people need sunlight?

"You don't look sold. Is it Elizabeth?"

Mark knew he had a reputation of inscrutability. Even Elizabeth had commented upon it. So there was no reason, no way, that Andrew should have noticed a tell on his face. Had he blinked? Had he winced?

"Don't look so surprised," Andrew said with a wry grin. "You're not the man of mystery you think you are. I know you."

Did he need to contribute verbally to this conversation at all? Apparently, his face was giving it all away. "There's no knowing whether things with her would work in the long-term. I can trust this opportunity."

"But not Elizabeth?"

Not himself.

"It's not that simple," he said instead.

"Have you prayed on it?"

Yes. No. "Not enough."

Mark had thanked God for this opportunity, but it had never occurred to him that God's plan might not involve him taking it. Could Elizabeth feature in his future if Mark found the bravery to risk his heart and livelihood and every vestige of security?

"I'd start there," Andrew said. "That's what I've been doing."

Before he could ask about what, his cousin was soaring forward again, carried along by the cold wind.

Heart sore, Elizabeth donned a dress for the rehearsal dinner—the one she'd originally planned to wear for the wedding before getting called in as a bridesmaid. Dark blue viscose flared around her waist, swaying down to her midcalf. The just-curled ends of her hair danced at its sweetheart neckline.

She looked beautiful. Put together. And all she wanted was to pull on her coziest pajamas and watch a Christmas movie with her parents. No rehearsal dinner. No difficult conversations with Mark. No excruciating conversation with Andrew. Just time with her family. How had this holiday become so focused on everything else? In three days, she'd head back to the city, and who knew when she'd be able to take the time off for another week at home?

The thought knotted her stomach with soured dread.

Unless…she didn't go back? Lowering herself to the edge of her bed, Elizabeth folded her hands onto her lap. She stared down at their winter dryness.

I don't know what I'm doing, Lord. There. That was a start. *I thought I was persisting on the path You'd set for me, but why do I feel so empty lately? Even before Mark.*

As much as it pained her to accept, Mark's decisions were his own. If he didn't want more from her than a wedding date and friendship, she would respect that. But her acting, her passion…

I was so happy at that show the other night. Happier than theater has made me in a long time. Thank You for helping me to understand Your plan for me, what You're leading me toward.

A line of scripture she'd read the other morning came to mind: *"For I know the thoughts that I think toward you, saith the Lord, thoughts of peace, and not of evil, to give you an expected end."*

Clasping her hands together again, tighter now, Elizabeth prayed for God's loving hand to help her toward that peace. So, Broadway hadn't starred in God's will for her yet. So, her plans from high school didn't resemble God's. How many people's did?

Elizabeth started listing off all that she had to be thankful for:

Thank You, Heavenly Father, for my loving parents. Thank You for our health and happiness. Thank You for how long my friendship with Tara has lasted, for the new hope in my friendship with Melissa. Thank You for the joy my dog brings me every day. Thank You for providing jobs that have fed and sustained me. Thank You for strengthening me each time an audition hasn't worked out as I'd hoped. Thank You for strengthening me now.

For a while longer, Elizabeth sat on her floral bedspread in silence, praying, meditating, seeking. She smothered the voice telling her to reach for her phone, to search for new auditions and opportunities. If she'd just throw herself into auditioning and work, she wouldn't have time to dwell on whether her life in New York still made her happy, now would she?

Bad logic.

If she left New York to restart here, to keep the Cranberry Players operating, would she succeed? Who was she to advise Herons Bay's children on acting?

Instead of allowing her anxiety to unravel further, Elizabeth looked inward and listened. *Help me, Heavenly Father, please.*

She didn't know. Not what was right, or what was next, or what to do besides listen for God's guidance. So, for just a few more minutes, she remained where she was seated and did exactly that.

Her phone chimed a few minutes later, interrupting her concentration. At first, she thought it was the alarm she'd set to remind herself to get going. Then she registered the wind chimes. She'd forgotten to turn that alarm off after her most recent rejection. Though she suspected she'd find spam or such at the top of her inbox, Elizabeth opened it anyway.

Her heart stopped. Resumed. Pounded. It did not appear to be spam.

Opening the email, scanning it, Elizabeth darted to her feet and pushed out of her bedroom. She knocked her knuckles against the door of her parents' room, praying they were home. A second later, her dad appeared in the threshold.

"Don't you look beautiful," he said. "Just like your mom at your age."

A cough sounded behind him, by the bed, where her mom was folding laundry—clean sheets and towels for the guests, it looked like.

"Just like your mom now, of course, as well," her dad added quickly.

"Thanks, hon."

Sweet as that was, Elizabeth's nerves and fingers were

jittering too much to accept the compliment or join their banter. Instead, she handed her phone over to him. "Will you read this for me? Please?"

Her mom abandoned her linens to join them by the door. "Is something wrong?"

Elizabeth didn't know.

"I think…I think I was just offered a part in a show. Not on Broadway, but…" A real musical. A real role. In a real New York City theater. "I tried out for this part a while ago and figured I wasn't going to hear back at all when I didn't get news. I'd almost forgotten about it, honestly."

"Lizzie!"

Her dad handed her phone off to her mom, engulfing her in a hug. Tears built behind her eyes. This was what she'd wanted. Good news to share with her parents. A Christmas miracle to revive her New York theater dreams. Wasn't it?

"It's a small part," she clarified. "But it could be big for me." Why then was excitement faltering into plain old nerves? *Because I was excited about the Cranberry Players. Because I was happy to think that I might be moving home.*

Her mom hugged her next. "We knew you could do it. This is so exciting! We'll have to celebrate after the rehearsal dinner."

No, she'd be celebrating by confronting her ex-boyfriend about his possible cold feet the night before his wedding. *Hurrah?*

"I think that might be a little late," Elizabeth said rather than unpack the favor Melissa had asked from her. "After the wedding?"

Though she had to head to the church, Elizabeth felt

herself walking over to her parents' sitting area instead. Plush hydrangea blue welcomed her. Her elbows dented the skirt of her dress as she put her head in her hands.

"Lizzie?" her dad said. "Everything okay?"

Looking up, Elizabeth found her parents standing over her, worry lining their brows.

"This wedding probably isn't how you'd choose to celebrate this news," her mom said. "We understand that."

"It's not that." Wringing her hands in her lap again, she forced her gaze up from her manicure to her parents. Their concern. Their love. "All I've wanted for so long now was an opportunity like this. To make you two proud, to prove that I deserved all your encouragement."

"You never had to prove that," her dad guffawed.

"We wanted this for you." Her mother's eyes held warmth. "Because you wanted it so badly. Don't you still?"

Elizabeth closed her eyes. Imagined returning to New York. Then she imagined not. "I found out that Cecelia and Harry are moving to Florida."

Her mom's mouth formed an O. "The Cranberry Players are closing?"

A nod. "I guess I thought God was nudging me to reconsider things. To maybe…move back here and try to take it over. You know how much that company meant to me. I'd hate for Herons Bay to lose it."

Her mom claimed the seat beside hers.

"But maybe that's not what God was telling me at all," Elizabeth continued. "Who gets an opportunity like this and turns it down?"

As her dad began to pace in short bursts across the living area, her mom took her hands in hers. Squeezed them.

"Put all that aside for a second," her mom said. "You have an email in your hand telling you that someone wants you to act professionally in a show. Breathe that in."

Elizabeth tried. She coughed.

"You have to appreciate everything God gives you before you can figure out what He wants you to do with it."

"What your mother said," her dad added with a smile.

"You're right," she said. "You're right."

How much time did she spend dwelling on what she didn't have? The auditions that didn't lead to roles, the job that didn't engage her passion, a trip home that was winding down bit by bit, day by day. A man who made her heart beam, who didn't want her.

Not much gratitude in there. Not any.

Mary Tyler Morkie had been curled up, asleep on a pile of laundry, but moseyed over to Elizabeth now, pawing at her leg. Beseeching her with her coffee eyes: *Lift, please?* She obliged, even though the clock was ticking ever closer to her departure time. Showtime. Mark.

"What do you think I should do?" She ran her fingers through MTM's coat as her eyes landed on her parents.

"We've always been proud of you. If you want this role, we'll be in the first row. If you want to figure out how to continue the Cranberry Players, we'll help however we can. I think you'd be marvelous. Even the other day, those kids had so much fun in that little play you put on with them. It looked like you did, too."

She had. Just like she missed the shows she'd help Ophelia and Juliet put on. Kids had so much enthusiasm, so much energy, so much joy—so much of what Elizabeth had longed for lately.

"And if you want to run away and join the circus,"

her dad input with a shiver, "I'll support you from afar. You know how I feel about clowns."

A smile spasmed across her mouth. As much as she wanted to joke back, to leave the stress weighing on her heart unsaid…"I figured, I don't know, that you'd want to be able to tell your friends that I'd made it in New York. That I wasn't delusional for still trying to act after college or ungrateful for not staying in Herons Bay."

The humor left her dad's face. "Listen to me. You did make it in New York. You've supported yourself in a very expensive city, you've juggled work and auditions and a life there, and we'll always be glad you chased your dreams. Herons Bay is here for you. That will never change, whether you move home tomorrow or in ten years."

Another squeeze of her mom's hand. "What your dad said. If you moved back, we'd be thrilled. Of course. But let it be because you *want* to, not because of us or other people in town or what anyone else thinks. We never want you to wonder, 'What if?'"

Elizabeth tried very hard not to cry; she wouldn't have time to fix her eye makeup before the rehearsal dinner if tears fell now.

"I love you both so much."

Her mom smiled. "Back at you, sweetheart."

Chapter Thirteen

It was the night before Christmas Eve, and Andrew and Melissa's wedding festivities had officially begun. The evening started with a simple rehearsal at the church, where they'd say their vows the following day. Where, tonight, Mark had walked down the aisle with Elizabeth in the procession. A vision in indigo, who was still icing him out with perfect kindness.

He didn't want her show smiles. He liked the true Elizabeth he'd seen over the past few days, not the Disney princess front. But that was all he'd gotten since she'd kissed him. Since he'd pushed her away. How could he blame her? He knew full well how rejected she'd felt this week, and he had gone and heaped onto the pile.

Nice one, Dr. Hayes.

His mom had it wrong. Elizabeth's sunshine had never burnt him, but he might get frostbite now from her guarded smiles. As if they'd never connected. As if she'd never kissed him. As if he'd never kissed her back.

No one to blame but yourself.

His gaze kept flickering to Elizabeth during the rehearsal, hoping to catch a crack in her performer's gloss.

None to be seen. After, he and Elizabeth had driven with his parents from the church to the restaurant, leaving no opportunity to talk then. Elizabeth had been peppy and friendly and had taken his dad's brisk answers in stride. A model fake date. Except it had stopped feeling fake to him somewhere between dinner one night and a show the next.

The rehearsal dinner followed. That Melissa and Andrew had rented out the private dining room at Sousa's Restaurant didn't surprise Mark. They'd gone with the tradition of the groom's family planning the dinner, and his aunt and uncle loved the steak here. But it disconcerted him, nevertheless, sitting next to Elizabeth in the very restaurant where she'd opened up to him just forty-eight hours ago. It would be easier if she were ignoring him or avoiding eye contact or being rude to him, even. At least then, he'd know where they stood. But she asked him if he'd found any books at Blue Heron earlier, then how his day had been, then how his steak was. Polite as can be, as if the slate between them had been wiped clean.

What was there to call her out on? Not acknowledging the moment he'd shut down? Not giving him her true smile, her real laughter? Would it have mattered if he did? Nothing seemed to break her composure. Not even the glances they'd garnered during the slide show of photos Phoebe had put together for Melissa and Andrew. Mark and Elizabeth had featured heavily in the "High School Years" section, with all its prom and homecoming snapshots.

Cue worried glances from his mom. Curious looks from Melissa and Andrew's college friends. Who knew why they cared. Who knew why they were here. Mark had always thought the rehearsal dinner was for the families and wedding party, but what did he know? He'd never been to a rehearsal dinner before.

He knew Andrew wanted him here. That meant more to Mark than he could have predicted. He realized now that it wasn't just Melissa or distance that had come between them—it was the suspicion that Andrew secretly agreed with his father. That Andrew also thought himself the superior cousin. And how could a friendship survive under that fear?

Clearly, it hadn't. But Mark hoped that could change now.

Speaking of things he'd like to change…

He turned to Elizabeth. "Can we talk?"

She faltered, finally, her smile slipping. "Here?"

He nodded toward the private dining room's exit.

Whether because she craved this conversation just as much as he did, or because she sensed he wouldn't drop it, Elizabeth rose to lead the way outside. The skirt of her dress flounced around her calves. Her waves bounced against her shoulder blades.

But there was nothing light or buoyant about the way she turned on him outside. Arms at her chest. Expression hardened with expectation. *Why am I outside in thirty-degree weather?*

A fair question. Mark cleared his throat. "Do you want my jacket?"

"No. No, I'm okay," she said, softening. "What did you want to talk about?"

There was too much to tell her. He started with, "I feel like I should apologize. The other night, I didn't…" *Didn't want to pull away from you. Didn't know how to tell you that I might be moving,* should *be moving, to*

*another part of the country in a couple weeks. Didn't
know how to tell you that, when I think about never seeing you again, my chest closes up. Don't know how to tell
you how terrified that reaction makes me because you
were never supposed to be this important... No one was.*

"Mark. It's okay. Really. I misread things and made a
mistake. You didn't do anything wrong. But I can't pretend it didn't happen."

"You didn't," he got out. Why hadn't he written her
a letter? A nice, clean piece of notebook paper he could
have filled with his thoughts, drafted and edited. Speech
was messier. "You didn't misread things."

She pushed her hair behind her ears, revealing their
pink tips. "It seemed like I did."

"I didn't want to ruin things between us. It seemed
easier to shut things down before we could both get more
invested. More hurt."

Elizabeth looked lost for words. Like he'd felt, faced
with her feelings.

"But I hurt you anyway. Myself, too. I'm sorry." Now,
he needed to tell her the rest, hammer the nail in the cof-
fin. "I should have told you yesterday, but I was offered
a position at a university that morning. In Chicago."

There. Done.

Elizabeth's face did several things in succession. Her
eyes widened. Her lips curved, even as they parted.
Dipped. Curved again.

"That's amazing. Congratulations."

Mark rubbed a hand against the back of his neck.
"Thanks. It's a temporary position, but it's an incredible
opportunity. You usually have to wait until late spring
for this kind of news. They need someone this semester to take over for a professor who had to take an un-

expected leave, though, and my doctoral advisor has a connection there. This doesn't happen."

"I'm really happy for you, Mark," she said softly. Sincerely, as far as he could tell.

She was being too nice. Too understanding.

"You're going to be an amazing professor. And I've heard great things about Chicago," she said, pulsing a palm around his upper arm.

"Windy things?" he joked.

"Those too." Her palm fell. The loss vibrated through him.

Why was his heart plummeting? He had everything he wanted—the job, the chance to explain himself to Elizabeth, her eyes making contact with his again. Why did his chest still ache?

"I actually got some good news, too," she said. "I got an email earlier letting me know I'd been cast in a show. A minor part, but—"

Before she could finish, before Mark could stop himself with thought or logic or reason, he was engulfing her in his arms. A hug. Just a congratulatory hug.

Laughter bubbled from her lips; he felt it in the crook of his shoulder. "Thank you?"

Mark pulled back, resisting the urge to avert his eyes. "They're lucky to have you."

The sight of Elizabeth brushing her palms and up down her forearms for warmth reminded him that it was time to go back inside. Back to the party and the heating and the curiosity of anyone who'd noticed their exit.

"I'm not sure I'm going to do it," Elizabeth said quietly. "That's unbelievable, right?"

Mark stared.

"I've wanted this for so long, but there's an opportunity here in Herons Bay, a gap in the community theater world that they're going to need filled, and I feel called to it."

Here in Herons Bay.

"I need to pray more on it. It's all pretty sudden."

Mark could relate to that. Clearing his throat, he said the only thing he was sure of. "You'll be great wherever you are."

After the other night, Elizabeth had no reason to ever kiss him again. To ever put herself out there with him again. But she rose to her tiptoes now and pressed her warm lips against his chilled cheek. Barely there. A ghost of a touch. He felt it down to his toes.

"I wish I'd known you in New York," she confessed. "Met you again there. Maybe we could have figured things out."

Mark swallowed. "Maybe."

And then she was walking back inside, and Mark was left to rub his suddenly aching head. If they'd had more time, could he have trusted that her feelings for him would last? Could he have truly found someone who would love him?

Reaching into his jacket pocket, Mark ran his thumb along the worry shell Elizabeth had found for him.

He trusted that this temporary job could become permanent, that the department could decide to keep him. Why couldn't he put the same faith in Elizabeth? In his value as a person as well as an academic?

As Mark pushed inside after Elizabeth, out of the cold wind, an idea began to knit itself together in his mind.

Chapter Fourteen

Andrew's front door loomed before Elizabeth like the entrance to a gothic mansion from a ghost story. Rather than what it was: the perfectly normal door to a perfectly pleasant-looking apartment building outside town. Once, this building had been a schoolhouse, but the only indication of that now was the Schoolhouse Apartments sign announcing itself to passing traffic.

Was this where she would live if she moved back? To start out, she'd probably move back in with her parents. The B&B would certainly have enough space for her during the dreary months of winter that followed December...

Elizabeth forced her finger to the buzzer for his unit. She didn't want to press it. Didn't want the door before her to unlock. Didn't want to do this at all. Though she'd texted Andrew earlier to let him know that Melissa had asked her to stop by after the rehearsal dinner on wedding business—though Melissa had assured her she'd told him as well—Elizabeth couldn't help but feel like a trespasser.

Hope had persisted all night that Melissa would have

changed her mind somewhere between Sweet Something and Sousa's. No such luck. When Elizabeth had said goodbye to her on her way out of the restaurant, Melissa had mouthed a *Thank you* to her with a meaningful look at Andrew.

So, here Elizabeth was. Never mind that she could still feel Mark's cheek on her lips. Never mind that she wanted to be talking to him right now, to know why he'd looked so sad as he told her his dream job had found him. If he felt the potential between them, too. If he thought she was foolish to consider turning down an opportunity on a New York City stage to return to Herons Bay instead.

She should be talking to Mark. And Melissa should be here, talking to Andrew. But Elizabeth pressed the buzzer anyway. Praying for God's guidance, she opened the screeching door and found the staircase that led to Andrew's apartment. *Thank You for helping me through this, Heavenly Father, for helping me find Melissa the clarity she needs.*

She knocked on the door quickly, as if it might zap her. Seconds later, Andrew answered. His glasses were in the process of sliding down his nose. Old paint stains smudged his long sleeves. His smile was the same he'd give a stranger.

"Elizabeth," he greeted, pulling her into a hug before she could step away. "Thanks for coming over." As if he'd invited her. As if she were here for a game night or Christmas cookie swap.

"Well, Melissa asked," she said, too sunnily, withdrawing from his arms.

"I'll admit," Andrew said as he ushered her inside, "she didn't tell me why, only that she wanted us to talk."

Elizabeth allowed her eyes to snap shut for a second. It was all on her to introduce the subject, then. How was she supposed to do that?

Stalling, she peered around his apartment. It didn't scream *bachelor pad* so much as *Andrew*: the bright artwork hanging on the walls, the handcrafted furniture strewn about.

"Can I get you anything?" Andrew asked, taking her coat from her shoulders. Elizabeth felt its removal like a crack in her armor.

No, thank you was on the tip of her tongue.

"A glass of water would be great," she said instead, her throat suddenly dry, her face growing hot. This wasn't her place. This wasn't her conversation. Melissa should be here. "Actually, never mind. I don't need water."

Andrew's face had creased in confusion. Elizabeth couldn't blame him. Taking him in, she got a good look at him for the first time in years. He hadn't changed all that much since high school, if you discounted the bit of roundness he'd lost in his cheeks, the muscles that had softened when he stopped playing lacrosse, but those changes had nothing to do with what a stranger he was to her now. She didn't know his heart anymore.

"This was a mistake," she breathed, reclaiming her coat.

"What was a mistake?" he asked, searching her face, raising a hand as if to brace around her shoulder only to drop it.

"Melissa asked me to talk to you," Elizabeth said. "But this conversation belongs between the two of you."

Alarm crossed his features, overtaking confusion. "Is she okay? She's not, is she? She won't tell me what's wrong…"

They were getting married. Tomorrow. They *had* to work on their communication.

"She doesn't think you want to get to married," Elizabeth said. "And she should really be telling you that herself, but she's too afraid. So, please, tell her that you do want to marry her and what's actually bothering you, because she's making herself sick with worry."

Slack-jawed. That was the only phrase that accurately described Andrew's face. It was almost cartoonish. "She doesn't think I want to marry her?"

Elizabeth held her hands up, message communicated. "That's why she asked me to come over here."

"She doesn't think I want to marry her, so she sent my ex-girlfriend over to chat about it?" he asked incredulously. "Right after our rehearsal dinner?" Almost to himself, he mumbled, "She's unbelievable."

Though his front door looked more appealing to Elizabeth than any other door ever had, defensiveness scaled its way up her throat. "She's scared. And you haven't shared whatever is actually on your mind with her."

"I didn't want to worry her." Andrew ran a hand through his light hair. "Ironic."

He sounded so earnest. Elizabeth tried to keep her tone gentle. "Then talk to her."

Obviously overwhelmed, he nodded. "I will. I want to marry her. None of this—it hasn't been about that."

"Good." Finally, she turned toward the door. "I'm not the one who needs to hear it, though."

More slow nodding, only for him to keep talking as if he hadn't heard her. "I can't wait for the wedding. But, after, we'll be buying a house, and it's a big—"

"Andrew," Elizabeth interrupted softly. "It's Melissa who needs to hear this. I should go."

"Right. Right." Another hand through his hair. "Who would've thought ten years ago that you'd be giving me relationship advice, huh?"

Not her. "I shouldn't have let Melissa talk me into this in the first place. She's just—"

"Hard to say no to," Andrew finished for her. "You know, I never felt that way with you."

"Like you couldn't say no to me?"

"Like you needed me to save you."

Elizabeth tried to smile at him. That was all well and lovely. Only. She had needed him the year they'd broken up, when she'd found herself homesick and struggling through freshman year. Maybe she hadn't been good enough at showing it. Or maybe he hadn't paid enough attention. All water under the bridge now.

"Good night, Andrew."

Elizabeth's only desire when she pulled up to her parents' house was to fall directly to sleep. It was that or stay up all night, obsessing over Mark and the wedding, and Mark and the email in her inbox awaiting a response, and Mark and the Cranberry Players. And Mark. The smoothness of his cheek beneath her lips tonight. The dead end looming before them.

Too much. It was all too much to consider at once. The whiplash of rejection and possibility. The two roads she could travel—neither of which traveled through Chicago, neither of which bisected with his.

Her heart hurt. Her bed beckoned. It was lucky, really, that she noticed the crisp white envelope tucked into the cranberry wreath hanging upon her parents' front door. For a guest? For her parents? It wasn't until she took it in hand that she noticed the name scrawled across its surface—her own.

Brennan.

Her aching heart began to race, her fingers to tighten around the envelope's edge. Careful to keep her footsteps light, Elizabeth hurried into the house and up to her bedroom. She opened the door gently, but Mary Tyler Morkie still heard her. She lifted her sleepy head up from the foot of her bed.

"Shh," Elizabeth said. Sitting on the edge of her childhood quilt, she scratched behind her dog's ears with one hand and held the letter with a death grip in the other. Her letter. Mark's letter.

Mary Tyler Morkie tilted her little head and then climbed directly onto her lap. As if she sensed the nerves spiraling through Elizabeth's chest, she started licking kisses onto her hand. Little cutie.

With a shaky breath, Elizabeth opened the letter— a basic legal envelope, plain white paper within—and began reading.

Dear Brennan,
I'm sorry to be writing you a letter. There was more I should have said to you tonight, more I should say in person to you now, but I didn't know how to start. Honestly, I don't know how to start this letter, either. Vulnerability has never been my strong suit. Here it goes.

I'm sorry (again). I'm sorry I made you feel like you'd done something wrong last night. I'm sorry that I shut down on you without warning. I'm sorry if I made you feel delusional for feeling a connection between us. You weren't. You deserve better than excuses, so I won't give them to you. I was responsible for my behavior. I could have told you about Chicago sooner. I could have admitted that I've thought about kissing you more than once this week.

Again, I've never been good at vulnerability. I have issues to sort out that have nothing to do with you.

When you first asked me out for coffee, I thought we'd suffer through some small talk, and that would be it. I didn't expect—well, I didn't expect you. I didn't think that my cheery high school rival would prove to be such a kindred spirit. I didn't expect that a night before the wedding, I'd dread never seeing you again. You're like a book I never want to stop reading.

I understand if you're wary of me. Or finished with me. That's your right. But I like you, Elizabeth Brennan, and I can't let this weekend pass by without telling you that. I wish I'd been brave enough to say this to you tonight. I hope I am tomorrow.

See you at the wedding, Brennan.
Yours,
Mark

Elizabeth did not get a wink of sleep that night.

Chapter Fifteen

Mark had expected more of a buzz in his parents' house the morning of Andrew's wedding. The way his parents had been anticipating it, anyone would have guessed they'd have headed over to Uncle Brad and Aunt Gina's house to enmesh themselves in every minute of the day-of preparations.

But when he walked downstairs that morning, he found them sipping coffee at the kitchen table as if it were any other Friday morning. His mom had her e-reader, his dad a sports news site pulled up on his tablet. Fresh-brewed coffee on the counter. Christmas music jittering through the stereo.

"Morning," he said, grabbing his oat milk from the fridge and pouring his own mug of coffee. A grateful gulp followed. Mark had only gotten a few hours of sleep last night. His mind raced through how he could fix things today. Wondering if Elizabeth had gotten his letter and read his scribbled words. What she was thinking, what she was doing, what she was feeling.

When he'd dropped it off at her house last night, relief had engulfed him. He hadn't seen her parents' car in the driveway. Maybe she'd needed a drive, solitude, time to clear her head after the rehearsal dinner. He sure had, but he figured she'd find the letter once she got home. Now, all he could think about was whether or not she'd seen it. Whether the wind had carried it away. Letters were romantic, but a Read notification would have put him out of his misery.

"Hard night?" his mom asked with a probing look at what he could only imagine were the very dark circles underlining his eyes.

"I had some things to figure out."

"About Elizabeth?"

How to answer that. Mark was about to try when his dad said, "Mark knows better than to expect more than a date from her."

Sometimes he took his dad's words too personally. Fine. But Mark felt justified in bristling now. He'd put his heart on the line; he didn't need his dad stomping on it before Elizabeth had a chance to respond. "Meaning…"

His dad looked up. "Come on, son. We've talked about this. She's heading back to New York. You're not exactly her type. Also—" a long sip of coffee, a deep breath "—this isn't easy to say, but I want you to hear it from me. One of my buddies saw Elizabeth leaving Andrew's apartment late last night. After the dinner."

A meaningful, pointed silence.

"She's in the wedding," Mark said slowly, wrapping his mind around this latest twist. That was where she'd been last night? Andrew's? "I'm sure she was there for Melissa."

Old insecurities pestered him, but Mark chose logic instead. Elizabeth didn't want Andrew. Andrew was in love with Melissa. There were any number of reasons

Elizabeth might have gone to see him last night, none of them incriminating.

Also. Elizabeth had kissed him. Elizabeth wanted him. Could she have gone to Andrew after Mark had rejected— *No.* No. He wasn't doing this.

"I just don't want you to get too invested with this girl. Not if she's still hung up on your cousin."

"They dated a decade ago," Mark said for what felt like the hundredth time this week, exasperation seeping into his tone from every conversation he'd had with his dad in recent years. "And Andrew's your golden nephew, isn't he? Why suggest something could happen between him and Elizabeth? The man is getting married tomorrow."

His dad coughed. "That's not what I meant to imply."

"Of course not. Because he's the son you've never had. And I'm the son you can't imagine a woman like Elizabeth choosing."

Pink suffused his dad's face. "Now, wait a minute—"

"No. I've borne the passive-aggressive comments and the digs and the comparisons to Andrew for years, and I think I've done so with grace. But I'm not going to take them anymore."

"Passive-aggressive?" his dad repeated, looking gobsmacked. "Digs?"

"Every time I'd call home from New York. Ever since I moved home. This whole time, I thought I did something to deserve it. And, sure, I'm not the sports fan that Andrew is, and I'm not as friendly and I'm clearly not the son you wanted. But you should still believe in me. You're my *dad*. You know, I was offered a position at a university in Chicago for this next semester, and I haven't told either of you because I couldn't handle hearing 'It's about time.'"

A first, Mark seemed to have stolen the words from his dad's tongue. Red-faced, his father stared at Mark like he'd never seen him before. And Mark supposed he hadn't, not like this. He'd never stood up to him before.

"Mark..." His mom exhaled, fingers white around her e-reader, voice paper-thin.

Rising, he squeezed her shoulder. Though he wanted to leave now, to let adrenaline carry him outside, he turned a level look on his dad. Waited to see if he'd reply. Apologize. *Acknowledge.*

But his dad remained silent, eyes cast down into his coffee. All right then.

"I'm going for a drive now," Mark said. "Please, don't go around spreading gossip about Elizabeth. And tell your buddy to stop, too. If not for me, then for Andrew. He doesn't deserve that right before his wedding."

And Elizabeth didn't deserve it all. Whatever reason she'd had for seeking his cousin out last night, Mark trusted its innocence. He was tired of living in his parents' doubt—of himself, of others, of the future.

His dad opened his mouth as if to respond only to close it again. Then a nod. Mark wished an apology would follow. An explanation. An assurance that he loved him. But his nod would have to do for now.

God loved him. God had good things in store for him. His dad didn't need to.

Elizabeth had attended some grand weddings in New York. She'd seen her college friends say their vows in ornate hotel ballrooms and on sunny Montauk beaches. None of those ceremonies compared to the embrace of her hometown church on Christmas Eve. What else could have pulled her thoughts from the letter she'd reread at least fifteen times last night?

That letter. Its words, etched into her brain, itched to fill her thoughts again. *A book I never want to stop reading. No. Not here. Refocus.*

After all Melissa's fear and fretting, her wedding day had proceeded without a single hitch. Phoebe looked radiant as her maid of honor, her hair twisted into an elaborate, braided bun, not a jet-lagged bag under either eye. Cecelia had played the harp beautifully enough to nearly bring Elizabeth to tears as her oldest friend walked down the aisle. She'd gotten a sneak peek at the cake Kristen had finished yesterday, frosted with snowy white buttercream, decorated with festive cranberries and pine cones.

As for the couple, Melissa was stunning. A vision in A-line ethereal white lace. Andrew hadn't taken his eyes off his bride since she'd walked into the church, not even when a baby started wailing in the back pew and needed to be carried outside.

Elizabeth gave silent thanks that they'd sorted things out. When she'd arrived at the Kents' house for hair and makeup, Melissa had taken her aside to offer a simultaneous thank-you, apology and update. It turned out that Andrew hadn't wanted to share his financial fears about house hunting with her. Meanwhile, Melissa had only needed to know he still wanted a life with her. And here they were now, about to embark upon their happily ever after.

If she weren't standing up here with the happy couple, cast in the role of bridesmaid, Elizabeth might have allowed herself to cry as they said their vows. As things were, she relied on years of acting to keep her composure. She'd spent too much time perfecting her eye makeup to muddle it before they took photos. So she blinked back her tears as Andrew slid a wedding ring onto Melissa's finger.

One second, her eyes were on that ring. The next, they were on Mark. *Mark.* So striking in his suit and emerald tie, a smile playing on his lips as he watched his cousin get married. So handsome. All day, she'd held him at the fringes of her thoughts to keep him from overwhelming them. Even now, as he stood beside Andrew and his best man, so close to her. So unreadable, though he could say the same of her. She hadn't talked to him since reading his letter. Last night, he'd cast Elizabeth's thoughts too asunder for her to gather them into a text message or a call. And today...

Well, today, she still didn't know what to say. Mark's letter was beautiful, but did it change anything? Could she trust that he wouldn't shut down on her again, even if they did find a way to make things work?

This morning, Elizabeth had talked to Cecelia and officially decided to move home and try to take over the Cranberry Players. She couldn't expect Mark to do the same.

A rebel tear stole down Elizabeth's cheek. God did everything for a reason. But she couldn't understand why He would have forged this connection between her and Mark just to sever it days later. Why He would call her to open her heart, to choose hope over fear, if Mark wouldn't do the same.

Elizabeth pulled herself back into the moment. Even if she never saw Mark again after this Christmas holiday, she had so much to be thankful for. The holiday decorations that filled her childhood church—poinsettias galore and garlands backdropping her friend's union. Out in the pews: her parents' teary eyes, Daisy's red-bowed ponytail, Kristen's brilliant smile—a new face in town who had saved the day by helping a virtual stranger. Even Melissa and Andrew's college friends, who couldn't seem to get over her romantic past with the groom at first, were beaming now. All brought together by love.

Home.

Elizabeth cherished it all as Melissa and Andrew said, "I do." A smile broke across Melissa's face when Andrew drew her into an eager kiss. Against her better judgment, Elizabeth's gaze strayed to Mark's again, drawn as though by magnets to his arresting ocean eyes. Was that longing she saw reflected in them? The same wish that pulled at her heartstrings? She looked away before she drowned.

The rest of the wedding passed in a blur—proceeding outside with Mark at her side, arranging for goose-bumped wedding photos in front of the church and Herons Bay's buoy Christmas tree. Mark's presence through it all, somehow all she could see or sense, even as she smiled for the photographer. It was half relief, half agony when the men were dismissed so the photographer could get a few photos of Melissa, Phoebe and Elizabeth alone. Easier to concentrate. Harder to breathe.

How was she supposed to say goodbye to him?

A hug from Melissa anchored her back into the present. "Thank you so much, Elle. For everything."

Swallowing her tears, Elizabeth hugged her back before they made their way into the reception. None of the baggage between them mattered today—not on Melissa's wedding day, not on a holiday that celebrated God's love,

Jesus's birth. Hopefully none of it would matter in the future, either.

"Of course. I'm so happy for you, Melissa. And Andrew."

When Melissa returned from her Vermont honeymoon, Elizabeth would tell her she was staying in Herons Bay. See if she might partner with her in taking over the Cranberry Players. Now wasn't the time, though, not with the reception calling. Literally. As soon as they reached its lawn, just a few doors down from the church, guests and music welcomed them into the Herons Bay History Museum. The building, an old federal-style house that had once belonged to a notable local whaling family, had transformed into a reception hall tonight—tables set throughout the room, a dance floor cleared, white lights twinkling about the space. Bouquet after bouquet of Melissa's favorite hydrangeas, all in a cardinal Christmas red.

Beautiful.

As a group of Kent cousins swallowed Melissa with cheers and hugs, Elizabeth made her way over to the refreshments table for a glass of hot cocoa. Bless Melissa's sweet tooth. Taking her place in line, she'd just started rubbing her chilled palms together when—

"Trying to warm up?"

Mark. Turning, she found him inexplicably at her side in the line for a hot beverage. The cold had touched his face, too, pinching his cheeks pink. Adorable. *Stop.*

"Outdoor winter wedding photos—beautiful but not for the faint of heart. Or the bare of arms," she joked.

"Here," Mark said, shrugging out of his jacket. Before she could wave off the gesture, he was setting it upon her shoulders.

"You didn't need to do that," Elizabeth said even as she nestled into the warmth of the coat. Mark's warmth. *Oh, Elizabeth.*

"You took a hundred photos in short sleeves. Only seems fair."

Elizabeth was about to wonder how he could remain so untouchable, so unreadable after everything he'd written to her when she noticed he wasn't. Those pink cheeks. That flushed neck. Mark was nervous.

He grabbed two mugs before she could reach for one and filled the first with holiday spice tea and the second with hot chocolate, topped by a mountain of marshmallows. Hers, she presumed.

She reached for the mug. "You don't have to do this, either."

His brow lifted as they looked for their table. "The marshmallows? I've seen you drink hot chocolate."

"Act like things are normal."

"Ah."

Well, now they certainly weren't. Elizabeth waited until they'd settled at their otherwise empty table to clear her throat. "You wrote me a letter."

Mark rested his elbows upon the table, all the better to lean closer to her. "I did."

"Very nineteenth-century of you," she said, voice wobbling, striving for levity and failing.

"I blame *A Christmas Carol.*"

Elizabeth went to push her hair behind her ears only to remember she'd styled it into a bun for the wedding. Her hands fell into a nervous knot on her lap. "That was the first handwritten letter of apology I've ever received. Thank you, Mark. Really."

Mark wrapped his palms around his mug of tea without taking a sip. Without looking away from her. "I should have said it all sooner. It's just…"

"Hard to talk about?"

A harder exhale. "Yeah."

Elizabeth curled her fingers into her dress's velvet. "Your letter meant a lot to me. These last few days have meant a lot to me, too. But I think you know that. There's… more I could say, but you're leaving and I—"

"I'm not."

It was a good thing Elizabeth hadn't taken a sip of her hot chocolate. She would have choked on it. He couldn't be saying what she thought. He couldn't be—

"I'm not leaving," he clarified.

Music and chatter abounded, but Elizabeth couldn't hear, either. The only sound to reach her ears was Mark's low voice.

He took her hand in his atop of the cranberry table-cloth. His eyes held hers as if locked by ice. "I'm sorry, Elizabeth. I shouldn't have pushed you away."

"I already told you," she said. "It's okay."

"It's not. I made you doubt yourself when I wanted exactly what you did."

He'd written this to her, but it felt different hearing it. His hand on hers, his mouth so near hers, as he said it. Elizabeth would have loved to reply, but her heart had leapt into her throat, blocking any and all speech. It was a blessing she could breathe. Was her palm sweating in his?

She watched his jaw work for his next words. "You might have noticed that my parents haven't always been the most supportive. My dad especially. The worst part is, I don't think he talks down to me out of cruelty or malice. He thinks he's looking out for me. Because he doesn't believe in me."

"Mark…" She breathed, before stopping herself. This was a time to listen.

"We have a lot to work on. For instance," Mark said, his voice gaining traction, "he doesn't seem to think I have a shot with you. That you could want someone like me."

"What?" she croaked. She could feel her eyes going doll-wide, could see her marshmallows dissolving in her untouched cocoa, but she couldn't move.

"I don't want him to be right. I've spent years pushing people away rather than risk disappointing them, closing myself off to keep my heart safe, and I barely even realized I was doing it until reconnecting with you. Even if you go back to New York, I want to see where this goes. I want to try."

For a moment, she couldn't speak, couldn't move. Then she said, "I'm not going back to New York," the words pouring out almost on top of each other. "Not permanently at least. I talked to Cecelia earlier today, and I'm coming home to take over the Cranberry Players as soon as I give my notice and find a subletter. I'm moving back."

A grin burst across Mark's face, all white teeth and wild joy, before he sobered again. "I know we have a lot to figure out. But…this is what I want. Not Chicago. I want to stay and see if we can make things work, because if I don't, I'll spend the rest of my life wondering. That job might be the safe choice, but I trust God has another plan for me. For us." A beat. "If you want there to be an us. I realize I'm presuming a lot here."

Faintly, she murmured, "But you wanted this job." And she couldn't let him give it up for her.

"I wanted a job like this one. And I'll find it. I still have applications in at schools in the area, and I'm going to trust that if I can get this offer, I'll find another. Before the wedding, I stopped by Blue Heron Books, and Alex and Annie agreed to take me on as a bookseller until then."

"Is that really what you want?" Elizabeth had to ask. An uncertain future? Herons Bay? Her? She couldn't let him make a spur-of-the-moment choice he'd come to regret. Only, Mark didn't do spur of the moment.

A firm nod. "When I think about moving to Chicago, I don't feel excitement over the position or the classes or the research opportunities. Not compared to the way I feel when I think about you."

Elizabeth swallowed. "And how do you feel when you think about me?"

He squeezed her hands tighter. "I feel like there are lots of jobs out there. And no one else like you in the whole world." A beat. "I think what I always have, Brennan. That you're perfect. It just doesn't drive me crazy anymore. What do you feel when you think about me?"

"I'm not perfect," Elizabeth protested. "And you... You're *Mark*."

"I'm Mark?" he echoed, hope tempting a half smile to his lips.

Slowly, Elizabeth felt herself nodding. Somewhere along the line, their chairs had moved closer together. Close enough that her chin almost brushed his when she said, "You're Mark, the man I'm falling in love with."

The words rose from her chest like a hot-air balloon, huge and unstoppable in their ascent. She'd promised herself earlier that she wouldn't share that, wouldn't risk compelling Mark to turn down an opportunity he needed to take, never mind her heart. But Mark didn't say things he didn't mean. And Mark, quite possibly, needed to hear someone else say they loved him first. She needed to be brave.

Before she had time to take another breath, Mark was tightening his hold on her hand and dipping his mouth to meet hers in a kiss. So fast, so soft. His lips landed on hers gently, reverently, impatiently. A contradiction. It consumed her every thought. It spoke of love even before he broke away and rested his forehead against hers to murmur it aloud.

"I'm falling in love with you, too. If that wasn't clear."

Elizabeth laughed. Or cried. Or both. Most probably, her eye makeup had gone to shambles. "I'm so thankful God brought you into my life."

"I guess," Mark said, almost dryly, mostly breathlessly, "we have to be thankful for this wedding, then."

Call it good timing, but just then, Elizabeth noticed snow pattering against the museum's tall windows, dusting the lawn white. Turning this moment into her very own snow globe.

A giggle exploded through Elizabeth's smile. She pressed another kiss to his cheek.

Epilogue

One Year Later

Applause spread throughout the seats of the Herons Bay Community Center's theater. Onstage, a cast of actors took their bows. *Her* actors. Her teens. Elizabeth beamed as the high school seniors, who had stayed from Cecelia's tenure as director of the Cranberry Players into her own, finished their holiday performance.

From a row behind her, her mom reached forward to place a supportive palm around her shoulder. Her dad gave a loud cheer. Mark's parents sat with them, more reserved in their applause but here. Trying. Their son had invited them to this Cranberry Players' production, after all.

A Christmas Carol. She'd been feeling sentimental. At her side, Melissa grinned at the stage. Who would have thought a year ago that Elizabeth would find herself working with Melissa, directing children of all ages in their favorite shows? And, hopefully by the summer, an original play of Melissa's own writing.

And, who would have thought, back in high school, that she and Melissa would be here today, with Andrew at Melissa's side and Mark at hers? Who could have predicted the Lord's plan?

Certainly not her.

After the show, she and Melissa rushed backstage to congratulate the cast. Christmas merriment abounded. The rush of performing, of absorbing an audience, of spreading joy through your art.

Elizabeth would say she missed it, but she was going to perform in a local production of *Into the Woods* this spring herself. It wasn't Broadway. It wasn't what she'd envisioned for herself at the age these kids were now. But she was *happy* working with kids again, entrenched in theater every day, home in Herons Bay once more. As for New York, Tara always welcomed her…and Mary Tyler Morkie.

Elizabeth couldn't stop smiling as she made her way out to the hallway, and her lips only stretched wider when she saw the tall, dark and handsome man waiting for her.

A large part of her happiness.

"Roses?" she said with a faux gasp. "Who could these be for? And wherever did you hide them during the show?"

"My girlfriend," he deadpanned. "And out in the car."

"Sounds like a lucky girl."

"Not as lucky as I am." A proud smile broke over Mark's features, rendering them utterly scrutable. "Elizabeth, that was…" he shook his head as if seeking the right words. Then he wrapped his arms tight around her, tucking the flowers against her back.

Laughter slipped from her lips. "Thank you."

"Amazing," he murmured into her hair. "They were amazing. You're amazing."

"Why, thank you, Dr. Hayes." What was really amazing was having him all to herself over the winter break. She'd gotten spoiled during his bookselling days, being able to stop into Blue Heron Books to see him whenever she liked. While he still picked up a shift here and there, for his love of books and the shop's owners, Mark was much busier now that he'd joined the English Department at a small liberal arts college squarely between Herons Bay and Boston.

"Do you want an autograph?" she teased as he pulled away. "Maybe a photo?"

Mark cleared his throat. Before she knew what was happening, he was falling onto one knee, gazing up at her with earnest unblinking eyes. "How about your hand in marriage?"

Vaguely, Elizabeth registered a chorus of *awws* and gasps sounding around them in the hall. All she could see was Mark. All she could hear was her own heartbeat and his question echoing in her head.

Reaching into his pocket, Mark pulled out a box. A ring box. This was *real*.

A sob broke from Elizabeth's chest. "Yes. Yes, yes, yes."

She dropped to her knees as well, cupping his face within her hands.

"You haven't seen the ring yet," he whispered.

He could propose to her with a Ring Pop, and she'd say yes.

"Yes," she said again. It was the only syllable she could find, the only one she wanted on her tongue.

Mark laid a kiss on her forehead. "Merry Christmas, Brennan."

As his ring—elegant and timeless and beautiful—slid onto her finger, Elizabeth thanked the Lord for this incredible man, this blessed Christmas, this boundless happiness bursting through her heart.

* * * * *

Dear Reader,

Thank you for joining Elizabeth and Mark in Herons Bay this Christmas season! I began working on their romance shortly after moving away from my family's hometown in Massachusetts. Though Herons Bay is not a real place, it draws upon all the towns across the South Coast and Cape Cod that I love so much. I hope you felt some of New England's magic among these pages.

Foremost, this is a novel about trusting God's plan. Elizabeth and Mark have dreams that they strive toward without any certainty they'll achieve them. Over the course of the book, they must choose those dreams over doubt, faith over fear, love above all else. Their journey resonated with me deeply, as it arose from a stretch of anxiety in my own life. Every morning, I would read a few verses from the New Testament for inspiration and then immerse myself within Elizbeth and Mark's story. It was a real comfort telling it and such a blessing to share it!

Thank you to Love Inspired for publishing my debut novel and to every reader who has chosen to pick it up. It's truly a dream come true, knowing my book is in your hands! Please feel free to keep in touch by visiting my website: KateKeedwell.com.

Merry Christmas!
Kate Keedwell

COMING NEXT MONTH FROM
Love Inspired

AN AMISH MOTHER FOR HIS CHILD
Amish Country Matches • by Patricia Johns

After giving up on romance, Verna Kauffman thought a marriage of convenience would give her everything she's longed for—a family. But marrying reserved Adam Lantz comes with a list of rules Verna wasn't expecting. Can they overcome their differences to discover that all they really need is each other?

HER SCANDALOUS AMISH SECRET
by Jocelyn McClay

A life-changing event propels Lydia Troyer to return to her Amish community to repair her damaged reputation—with a baby in tow. And when she finds old love Jonah Lapp working on her family home, she knows winning back his trust will be hardest of all...especially once she reveals her secret

FINDING THEIR WAY BACK
K-9 Companions • by Jenna Mindel

Twenty-eight years ago, Erica Laine and Ben Fisher were engaged to be married...until Erica broke his heart. Now, as they work together on a home that Erica needs to fulfill her new role as a traveling nurse, their past connection is rekindled. But can love take root when Erica is committed to leaving again?

FOR THE SAKE OF HER SONS
True North Springs • by Allie Pleiter

Following a tragedy, Willa Scottson doesn't hold much hope for healing while at Camp True North Springs. But swim instructor Bruce Lawrence is determined to help the grieving widow and her twin boys. This is his chance to make amends—if Willa will let him once the truth comes out...

THE GUARDIAN AGREEMENT
by Lorraine Beatty

When jilted bride Olivia Marshall is forced to work with her ex-fiancé, Ben Kincaid, it stirs up old pain. Yet she finds herself asking Ben for help when her four-year-old nephew is abandoned on her doorstep. Will their truce lead to a second chance...or will Ben's past stand in their way?

SAVING THE SINGLE DAD'S BOOKSTORE
by Nicole Lam

Inheriting his grandfather's bookstore forces Dominic Tang to return to his hometown faced with a big decision—keep it or sell. But manager Gianna Marchesi insists she can prove the business's worth. Then an accident leads to expensive damages, making Dominic choose between risking everything or following his heart...

LOOK FOR THESE AND OTHER LOVE INSPIRED BOOKS WHEREVER BOOKS ARE SOLD, INCLUDING MOST BOOKSTORES, SUPERMARKETS, DISCOUNT STORES AND DRUGSTORES.

LICNM1123

Get 3 FREE REWARDS!

We'll send you 2 FREE Books plus a FREE Mystery Gift.

FREE
Value Over
$20

Both the **Love Inspired**® and **Love Inspired**® Suspense series feature compelling novels filled with inspirational romance, faith, forgiveness and hope.

YES! Please send me 2 FREE novels from the Love Inspired or Love Inspired Suspense series and my FREE gift (gift is worth about $10 retail). After receiving them, if I don't wish to receive any more books, I can return the shipping statement marked "cancel." If I don't cancel, I will receive 6 brand-new Love Inspired Larger-Print books or Love Inspired Suspense Larger-Print books every month and be billed just $6.49 each in the U.S. or $6.74 each in Canada. That is a savings of at least 16% off the cover price. It's quite a bargain! Shipping and handling is just 50¢ per book in the U.S. and $1.25 per book in Canada.* I understand that accepting the 2 free books and gift places me under no obligation to buy anything. I can always return a shipment and cancel at any time by calling the number below. The free books and gift are mine to keep no matter what I decide.

Choose one: ☐ **Love Inspired Larger-Print**
(122/322 BPA GRPA)

☐ **Love Inspired Suspense Larger-Print**
(107/307 BPA GRPA)

☐ **Or Try Both!**
(122/322 & 107/307 BPA GRRP)

Name (please print)

Address   Apt. #

City   State/Province   Zip/Postal Code

Email: Please check this box ☐ if you would like to receive newsletters and promotional emails from Harlequin Enterprises ULC and its affiliates. You can unsubscribe anytime.

Mail to the Harlequin Reader Service:
IN U.S.A.: P.O. Box 1341, Buffalo, NY 14240-8531
IN CANADA: P.O. Box 603, Fort Erie, Ontario L2A 5X3

Want to try 2 free books from another series! Call 1-800-873-8635 or visit www.ReaderService.com.

---

*Terms and prices subject to change without notice. Prices do not include sales taxes, which will be charged (if applicable) based on your state or country of residence. Canadian residents will be charged applicable taxes. Offer not valid in Quebec. This offer is limited to one order per household. Books received may not be as shown. Not valid for current subscribers to the Love Inspired or Love Inspired Suspense series. All orders subject to approval. Credit or debit balances in a customer's account(s) may be offset by any other outstanding balance owed by or to the customer. Please allow 4 to 6 weeks for delivery. Offer available while quantities last.

Your Privacy—Your information is being collected by Harlequin Enterprises ULC, operating as Harlequin Reader Service. For a complete summary of the information we collect, how we use this information and to whom it is disclosed, please visit our privacy notice located at corporate.harlequin.com/privacy-notice. From time to time we may also exchange your personal information with reputable third parties. If you wish to opt out of this sharing of your personal information, please visit readerservice.com/consumerschoice or call 1-800-873-8635. **Notice to California Residents**—Under California law, you have specific rights to control and access your data. For more information on these rights and how to exercise them, visit corporate.harlequin.com/california-privacy.

LIRLIS23

HARLEQUIN PLUS

Try the best multimedia subscription service for romance readers like you!

Read, Watch and Play.

Experience the easiest way to get the romance content you crave.

Start your **FREE TRIAL** at
www.harlequinplus.com/freetrial.